High-Speed Chase

"Run it!" Tumbler yelled.

"Damn!" Kip floored it straight for the middle, hoping it was something like bowling a seven-ten split, where he knew he'd probably only hit one. The cops had time for a few shots, and one wild, over-the-shoulder throwaway got lucky, drilled the windshield, and came to rest in Toby's shoulder. The Cadillac swerved onto the grass median, through a road sign, and back onto the road on the other side. Kip punched the gas, getting them out of there.

"Just hold on, Toby," Kip said, seeing his shirt and the spreading stain of blood. "Please. Just hold on."

Gone in
60 Seconds

Gone in 60 Seconds

A NOVEL BY
M. C. Bolin

BASED ON THE SCREENPLAY
WRITTEN BY
Scott Rosenberg

HYPERION
NEW YORK

Book design by Ruth Lee

ISBN: 0-7868-8989-6

FIRST EDITION

1 3 5 7 9 10 8 6 4 2

Gone in
60 Seconds

1

He was back in Long Beach, in dreamlike Los Angeles, ambling up an empty sidewalk on northbound Ocean Boulevard on a Sunday morning, and there she was.

A 1967 Shelby Mustang GT-500. Satin nickel paint job, deep-set, shark-profile grill, and sculpted side panels, parked at the curb. She was beautiful.

He was Randall "Memphis" Raines, dark hair, medium build, black turtleneck, black leather duster, jeans, boots—at twenty-three, the best car boost in Southern California.

They were made for each other.

"You gonna steal her or kneel down to her and pray?" someone said.

The voice came from the street. Memphis turned at once to see another car rolling up—a 1990 Ford Thunderbird. Ice blue, chrome racing wheels, blackout glass, thundering bass in the trunk, its driver grinning bone-white teeth at the open passenger-side window. It was Atley Jackson.

Black, handsome, late twenties, jocular, black T-shirt, black leather jacket, black sunglasses. In the car's black leather interior he looked like an angel from the dark side out on parole, cruising around sunny L.A. and seeing the sights.

You gonna steal her or kneel down to her and pray?

The T-bird's power window went up like a curtain closing, and the car rolled away in the downtown direction. Atley wasn't waiting for any kind of answer from Memphis, really. No need. They knew each other all too well.

Memphis checked the street in both directions. It was deserted, even for Sunday morning. He pulled a small "slim jim" from his coat (never left home without it), a handy door-opening tool popular among uniformed police officers, AAA service representatives—and yes, car thieves.

He slimmed the door panel, popping the lock from underneath the button, opened the door, and got into the bucket seat behind the wheel. He ran a cordless screwdriver over the dress panels around the steering column, thus revealing the ignition's lock cylinder. Finally he pressed a small, socketlike device known as a "gizmo" into the key slot, and with a twist of the wrist, the 320-bhp 289 V-8 engine rumbled like a jackhammer.

What's this—no seat belts? You could get a ticket for that. Oh, well. He pushed a cassette tape into the deck, and Bruce Springsteen's "Ramrod" wailed from the coaxials.

And then he floored it.

Tires screaming, engine roaring, the smell of asphalt in the morning—these were a few of his favorite things. He had the needle halfway around the speed dial, halfway to the charge of super-satisfaction and well-being known locally as an Ocean Boulevard speed rush. Here came the sun, and the birdies were flyin'. *Welcome to L.A.! Have a nice day!*

Two unmarked South Bureau cop cars briefly spotted Memphis jetting through some intersection—too quick to tell which one. They slapped magnetic bubble-flashers on their roofs and called in a Code Three (emergency, use lights and siren)—pursuing a 510 (speeding vehicle), possible 503 (stolen), traveling south on O.B.

Memphis checked them in the rearview, carved a right, and punched the accelerator again. He raced the Shelby toward the Pacific Ocean, down the early-morning, harbortown streets now echoing with the woeful siren cry.

Turning north again, he encountered a two-cycle delay backed up at the light and gutterballed around it, skating the shoulder. A new pursuit car slipped into his wake—the South Bureau operations dispatch was broadcasting a chase report on an open channel, and now every cruiser in the harbor area was in on the act, closing the net.

The trap itself was set for an on-ramp to the Terminal Island Freeway. They herded him there, never doubting the suspect's intentions to outrun them and then stow the car under a bridge or in the parking deck of a mall in the back-country suburbs. It would wait there, tucked between mothers' minivans, for the truck from the chop shop to come.

Traffic control had a detour in progress and two aging cruisers nose to nose like a gate in the ramp. A news traffic copter was on the scene too, ready to put the live feed on TV.

A lucky cruiser met him head-on and flashed its headlights, spooking him in exactly the intended direction. He swerved onto the entrance ramp, pedal to the metal, aimed point-blank at the roadblock. Uniformed officers scattered as he gunned it, then at the last possible second, he bailed out—banged the gearshift into neutral and yanked the parking brake, putting her into a spin, popping her up the curb, and flipping her over the guardrail and into a side roll in the path of something with an air horn, coming on like a locomotive.

He screamed—

—and woke up in a cold sweat.

It was a dream. Only a dream!

The nightmare was still to come.

2 What truly distinguished the 1990 Trans Am tracking up the street was not the sparkle from the paint job, the slickness in the sidewalls, or the throaty rumble of the tailpipe. What distinguished it was the bare fact that it had managed to go a half mile through upscale Beverly Hills without the cops even once curbing it for a dope search. Or, as it was known in more polite circles, "a license check."

The car had two occupants in front and one in back. Behind the wheel was Kip Raines, built for surfing, cocky and glowering. Riding shotgun was the unobtrusive Freb, a complacent number-two man who found contentment traveling life's highways in Kip's shadow. In the backseat was "Mirror Man," who was named after his sunglasses. In their twenties, Kip, Freb, and Mirror Man had crossed into the years of peak production for their chosen craft. By the time they reached thirty, most car thieves were either retired by the government or dead.

The Trans Am pulled over into a pool of light softly spilling from an exhibition of astronomically priced cowboy clothing. Freb checked their instructions, hastily scribbled on the inside wrapper of a torn cigarette package.

"The corner of Wilshire and Wetherly. Tumbler messed up," Freb said. Tumbler, a partner in the firm, had provided the directions to the client. "He said the Porsche would be at the corner of Wilshire and Wetherly."

Nothing like a Porsche was parked at the corner of Wilshire and Wetherly.

Then Kip's hand on the wheel pointed a finger at a building taking up the corner across the street. "He didn't mess up. There it is."

Behind the twenty-foot-high, glass showroom window of a Porsche dealership on the corner of Wilshire and Wetherly. That's what Tumbler had meant. The car they had come for, a new 996 Aero Coupe, turned slowly behind the glass on a revolving platform, reminding Kip of Thanksgiving Day at Mom's house—dinner on the rotisserie. The car gleamed in the all-night showroom lights.

"That?" Freb said.

"You're shittin', right, Kip?" Mirror Man said.

Kip answered with a grin, then said, "I need my tool." He popped the trunk, got out, and went around back. Freb and Mirror Man traded puzzled looks.

What Kip meant was that he needed a brick.

"Oh, no," Mirror Man said.

Calm and cool, Kip went to the curb in front of the windows, wound up, and hurled the brick through the safety-glass door, which exploded, showering glass like champagne spray under the showroom lights. Alarms squealed as Kip stepped inside, through the crumbs of glass. Freb and Mirror Man were visibly impressed.

Inside, Kip jimmied the key box at the receptionist's desk, removed a handful of ringed sets with yellow paper tags stamped *Showroom*, and took them over to the Aero Coupe on the turntable. He found the VIN—vehicle identification number—stamped into a small metal plate on the car's dashboard visible through the windshield, matched it to the right showroom tag, and dropped the rest of the keys to the floor.

They only needed one car.

He used the keys to open the coupe, started it, and Mirror Man climbed in on the passenger side. "How we supposed to get outta here?" he asked Kip.

This was no off-road vehicle; the seats were firm, spare, and low to the ground, the chassis practically kissed the road, and even if they could somehow get the car off the turntable, the windows wrapped them in, all around the showroom. Never mind the two-foot drop to street level.

"You expectin' to fly?"

Kip grinned, revved the engine, and set his eyes dead ahead.

"Oh, no," Mirror Man said. "You ain't gonna—"

Kip floored it, striping the turntable with rubber lines, skated across the polished floor all the way to the windows—and went right through them.

The car slammed onto the sidewalk, rebounded on its shocks, then gyrated into the street, barely missing a passing car. Kip forced the wheel over, regained control, then peeled up Wilshire Boulevard with Freb in the Pontiac chasing his smoke.

"News flash, Kip," Mirror Man said, enjoying the ride now. "You're driving a stolen car!"

"Stolen *fast* car," Kip corrected, downshifting for a light. A half hour later, as they neared the Long Beach warehouse that was their rendezvous point, Kip rolled the coupe to the paint and discovered a starlet blonde in a black Honda Prelude by his side. She looked over, pushed the stick shift forward into first, and gunned the engine. Whoa! It looked like she wanted to race!

The light turned green and Kip popped the clutch. Both cars pulled away hard, and Kip had to smile over at the blonde. Mirror Man was freaking out.

"They say this thing can do one-seventy!" Kip hollered. "Should we test it out? Should we have a party?"

Mirror Man's hands squeezed the dash. "Don't do it, Kip! Don't do it!"

Too late. Kip did it. He floored it, and even though the cars stayed neck and neck to the speedometer's century mark, after 110, the Porsche pulled away.

He was pushing 140 when they passed the cop.

Officer Bill Figilis was an experienced uniformed cop in the LAPD's Office of Operations, the department responsible for several important duties: one, to stimulate mutual understanding between the police and the community to prevent crime; two, to patrol the streets to prevent crime; three, to identify and arrest criminal offenders; four, to recover stolen property; five, to enforce traffic laws; and six, to advise the public in an emergency situation.

Kip Raines was giving him an opportunity to score points in all six categories with a single arrest.

He put down his coffee cup and called the South Bureau dispatcher on the squad car's CB. "I've got a silver Porsche doing a buck-forty west on Long Beach Boulevard," he said. He pulled out, then lurched to a stop as Freb blew past in the Pontiac.

The dispatcher relayed an alert for both cars. It was received by a police helicopter pilot, who spotted the Porsche on the Long Beach Bridge and swept along behind it like a hawk tailing a rabbit.

A scant mile from the bridge, at a warehouse on the harbor, was Tumbler, Kip's boyhood chum, a ripe old twenty-one years of age. He studied his watch, a little concerned. He shot a glance at Atley Jackson, who was staring at him.

"Something wrong, Tumbler?" Atley said.

"Yeah," Tumbler replied. "I'm missing *Springer*—" But he stopped at the sound of a car horn. It was Kip and Mirror Man, bringing the Porsche up the loading ramp and into the warehouse. Tumbler flashed Atley an I-told-you-so smile as Kip and Mirror Man emerged from the little car.

Tumbler went to a plastic ice chest. He raised the lid and passed out forty-ounce bottles of beer in a celebratory manner.

"Thirteen down," he said, as a toast. "Thirty-seven to go."

Cars. Fifty of them. High-ends and exotics. It was a big order, even for Long Beach, where the movement of cars both inside and outside jurisdiction was big business. For Kip, who ran the operation, it was a chance to prove himself. "No problem," he said of the thirty-seven remaining to be boosted. "How ya doin', Toby?" he asked the kid, who was watching the toast.

"It's all good," said the kid, at sixteen still an apprentice learning the ropes.

The crew clinked bottles and turned them up. Kip thought about Freb, still due with the other car. He shot a glance through the open overhead door to the loading dock, the turnaround, and the driveway beyond it, expecting headlights, maybe. But some other light swept by—not headlights.

A *spotlight.*

Kip, Mirror Man, Tumbler, Toby, Atley—everybody looked like zombies in the white-hot spotlight that bored through the warehouse skylight. Then they felt the rapid drum of helicopter rotors and heard the wail of police sirens closing in.

Outside the warehouse, the Los Angeles Police Department was converging on the building.

It was time to break up the party.

"Now you've done it, Raines!" Atley yelled. "Somebody get the board!"

Tumbler was already wiping the list of car names off the board with his shirtsleeve. Spotlights in the windows were turning the warehouse into a stage scene. Tumbler panicked, smashed the black-light bulb that illuminated the board with his fist, rendering the marker lines invisible, and sprinted away.

The turnaround beside the loading dock was becoming a parking lot for police vehicles, cruisers and wagons manned by uniformed officers. A Lexus SUV arrived, carrying detectives, the traditional follow-up to the raiders.

First out of the passenger side was Detective Roland Castlebeck, a cop's cop—tough, dedicated, and effective. The driver of the vehicle was his partner, Detective Drycoff, less experienced than Castlebeck, but perceptive and shrewd. The men were out of the Operations Headquarters Bureau, which served South and the other districts with investigative service. Their department, Detective

Services, was a bureaucracy of specialized units organized by criminal activity. Castlebeck and Drycoff's unit was Burglary/Auto Theft. Due to a recent increase in stolen vehicles, BAT had formed a special task force known internally as GRAB—the Governor's Regional Auto-theft Bureau.

Drycoff entered the warehouse ahead of Castlebeck to get the on-the-scene report from the uniforms, while Castlebeck surveyed the room, doing a walk-through with his hands instinctively held behind his back, preserving the evidence.

"Anybody?" Castlebeck asked when he saw Drycoff off by himself. He was looking out at the dock. The first police units had backed off the scene for the investigators, but a few lingered in the parking lot. The reflections of their blue lights oscillated on the hull of a freighter in the harbor.

"All gone. We didn't get one of them."

A camera flashed. The warehouse and the vehicles were being photographed and measured. A fingerprint man was already dusting the obvious—doors, steering wheels, beer bottles. The police had recovered thirteen vehicles, a good night's work, but the real questions were yet unanswered. Who were the cars for? Was this the entire order? And who was doing the boosts? Castlebeck's eyes went to three Mercedes sedans, all brand new.

"We're talking professionals," Drycoff said. "There's no visible damage to locking mechanisms, steering columns, or ignitions. And these aren't Honda Accords. Those new Mercedes? They're supposed to be unstealable."

Castlebeck automatically did a rewind, imagined the scene, the vehicle, and the perpetrator, and mentally watched the crime unfold like viewing a short film in his head. "Say the suspects have laser-cut transponder keys, sent here direct from Hamburg. Dealer keys."

Drycoff backed it up a step. "They paid off somebody working the inside. Somebody on staff at a car dealership."

It made sense. "Find out which dealership sold these, serviced them, et cetera," Castlebeck said.

Drycoff made a note. "I'm on it."

Then Castlebeck spotted a thin, curved shard of blue glass on the floor. He toed it with his shoe, then bent and picked it up. It glinted in his hand.

He dropped it into his coat pocket.

"Impound the cars," he told Drycoff. "One month. I don't give a rooty-toot if they belong to Tom Cruise. Dust them, and dust every inch of this pigsty."

"This would have been a pretty big score, you know?" Drycoff said. "And yet I heard you ran all the big dogs out of town. No one's tried a score this big since—"

"Yeah, I know," Castlebeck said. "Six years ago."

Four hundred miles to the north, in the little town of Independence, engines whined. Not like the Porsche, though. Thinner and higher, because they were smaller.

Go-karts.

3

For the life of him, he could not remember when he had spoken to a more canny and perceptive audience. Memphis Raines could tell anyone how to *drive*—but this group was onto something more heady, the very *soul* of driving:

Racing.

"Acceleration, speed, and emotional self-pacing—these are the three fundamental components of the new generation of race car driver," he told them. "Unpredictability and adrenaline are the by-products, but remember: To drive is to feel; to race is to live."

Twenty uniformed and helmeted kart racers in the six- to eight-year-old age group regarded him with utter awe. To them, his words were like mantras. "Let's ride," he told them.

Out on the track, a seven-year-old accelerated into a turn, the five-horse Tecumseh engine screaming like a bee. "That's it!" Memphis cried. "Don't ride the brake! Good! Good!"

A Black Fox All-Terrain kart spun out and landed on its side near the surrounding wall and Memphis ran over and crewed for the boy driving, straightening out the kart. "Tommy, I don't know what that was," he said, "but it wasn't driving."

Beyond the fence, a dark Cadillac with tinted windows pulled through the gravel parking lot and came to rest near the gas station that fronted the kart track. The driver's-side door opened, and out like a wraith emerged Atley Jackson, in a long leather coat, dragging on a cigarette. In apple-pie Independence, here was the worm. He sauntered over to the kart track and took a seat in the bleachers.

"Well, well, well. What do you pay your pit crews—Oreos and gummy bears?"

Memphis looked up and acknowledged the remark with a strained smile. He finished wrapping a Band-Aid around a driver's cut finger and focused his attention on his visitor.

"Hello, Atley," Memphis said. "How's the leg?"

Atley cupped his bony hand around his right thigh, just above the knee. "Only hurts when I breathe. And when I drive six hours straight just to see you. What the hell are you doing, boy-o?"

Memphis raised his hands at his sides, palms up, and Atley took it all in: the blue sky, the old-time gas station (with Raines's name on the sign—Raines Auto), the little kart track, the kids.

"Woo-hoo! This is livin'," Atley concluded. Then he gave Memphis a hard, questioning look, as he would an impostor. "You been gone how long now?"

"Six years," Memphis reminded him, and because he and Atley had a history, he felt the need to show something for it. "Some of these kids are pretty good. See Billy over there? The one with the red helmet? We're taking him to the California Junior Invitational."

Atley nodded, but it was clear he measured things differently. "Six years of bake sales and bingo. How do you survive?"

It suddenly occurred to Memphis that Atley wasn't owed an explanation, that he probably wouldn't understand anyway. "You'd be surprised at how good it is, not to have to worry about a bullet in my back or a cop in my cupboard." That was enough. "Now, what are you doing here?"

"Is there someplace we can talk?"

"What about?" Memphis couldn't imagine anything in Atley Jackson's world that would matter to him anymore. But he was wrong.

21

"It's about your brother," Atley said, "and the deep shit he's in."

In the single-bay garage fronting the go-kart track Memphis pulled two root beers from an old glass-bottle vending machine, cracked the tops in the built-in opener, and handed one to Atley. The man took a pull and then turned and goof-walked to the pumps, whistling the *Andy Griffith* theme. The small-town atmosphere struck him as funny. He pulled a handle from the pump and said, Gomer Pyle–style, "Hey, Andy! Where's Aunt Bea and Opie hanging out at?"

Memphis just smiled and shook his head. Atley hung the pump up and returned to the garage bay, grinning. "Haw! Are you kidding me, man?"

"Tell me about Kip," Memphis said.

Atley quieted down, took another swig of root beer, reached inside his coat for a cigarette, then changed his mind. All of this was only meant to put off the final act of bringing Memphis the bad news.

"He took a job. And he fumbled it. Now he's jammed up. Jammed up bad."

"A job? What kind of job?"

"A boost," Atley told him. "A big boost."

"A boost?" Memphis's eyes narrowed. "What's Kip doing on a boost?"

"You're shittin', right? You don't know? Kip's become quite the little crew-runner since you left. He's been working a low-rent ring for two years now. You don't talk to your ma?"

Memphis felt knocked down. "It seems she neglected to mention it."

Atley shook his head. "The point is, Kip's been living the life. Only he's a wild child. Crazy. Makes our old behavior seem like altar boy time. But he fungoo'd this one so bad, folks around L.B. are already speakin' about him in the past tense."

"Who was the job for?" Memphis wondered if he might have some influence. Six years was a long time, but he still knew people.

"New guy. Brand new. Moved in a year ago. Raymond Calitri. They call him 'The Carpenter.' Running all the dark ponies in town. It's the full-on, 'Devil Came Down to Long Beach' trip, man. He's bad. Real bad."

"And this Calitri's after my brother?"

"Like stains on a mattress. And you should know: I work for him."

Memphis gave Atley the look he deserved for that.

"Hey—there weren't a lot of opportunities for retired car thieves on the gimp. He put me to work. But I gotta tell ya, Memphis . . . this guy? He scares the shit outta even me."

Memphis nodded, fully understanding.

The joke around the shop at Long Beach's Exeter Salvage and Steel was that if you pissed into the hydraulic crusher when they were doing a Mercedes, you got Becks in cans, and even if it was just a joke, it said a lot about the power of the machine that inspired it.

The night of the same day that Atley went to Independence, the boys at Exeter were getting ready to do a Trans Am. It was after hours, but if you asked any of the crew, it was worth staying up for. This was going to be a unique crush. The vehicle's owner, Kip Raines, would be in the driver's seat, handcuffed to the wheel.

"Calitri!" Kip yelled through the bruises on his face. "We can work this out! Think about what the hell you're doing!"

Calitri, early fifties, wearing the kind of clothing you saw pictured in woodworking magazines—

pressed, immaculate overalls, starch-white shirts—
believed he knew what the hell he was doing, all
right. He was applying to Kip the "no pain, no
gain" principle that was the foundation of the Calitri empire—no pain for you, no gain for Calitri.

Kip's car was cradled in the blades of a forklift, poised over the crusher's ramming chamber.
He nodded to the forklift operator, and the boom
tilted the car in, blowing the airbags, pinning Kip
to the seat.

"Gimme a second chance!" Kip screamed,
muffled behind the airbags.

Calitri heard him. "Were it only that easy," he
said quietly, and nodded again. The crusher motor
squealed and the ram gave the roof columns a new
set of elbows. The top collapsed and the firewall
caved in, snapping the steering column. Kip's eyes
widened in terror; desperately he tried to force the
door open.

"Listen, Calitri!" he screamed.

Kip's terrified voice was drowned out by the
sound of his car's steel panels undergoing reconfig-
uration in the crusher.

"Call me Ray," Calitri shouted over the noise,
and raised his hand for the operator to stop. "Better
yet, call me 'asshole,' because that's how you've
treated me!" he yelled. Then he nodded, and the

crusher stole another couple of cubic feet from the car's interior.

"Calitri!" Kip cried out.

Memphis and Atley came down from Independence in Atley's car and went around the city, picking up the 110 on the south side and taking that straight into Long Beach. When they had entered Long Beach proper, Atley made a call on his cell phone, then hung up, face grim.

"They have Kip right now," he said.

"Take me there," Memphis told him.

Atley steered the car through a maze of streets and alleys in the West Basin until they came to a vast yard of automobile carcasses. They pulled up to a salvage yard where a sign by the garage warned:

> **LOCK YOUR CAR**
> **OR IT MAY BE GONE IN 60 SECONDS!**

Atley parked, and Memphis followed him through the building to a three-thousand-square-foot, state-of-the-art woodworking shop—saws, drill presses, planers, a jointer, and a deep inventory of high-grade, quartersawn hardwoods and rare and endangered exotics: Brazilian kingwood, ebony, olivewood, pinkwood, teak, and pear. Chemicals were stored in neat cases against the back wall—jars, bottles, and cakes of glues, resins, oils, paints, stains, bleaches, waxes, varnishes, putties, strippers, thinners, and cleaners.

At one of the benches, a trio of young fops were flirting with a lovely blonde.

"Well, well," said one of the boys. "It's Atley, and he's brought a friend."

"Gentlemen," said another, introducing the girl, who was on his lap. "Say hello to Tami." Then to her, "Give us a minute, would you, love?" and she sidled off.

Passing close to Memphis, she said, "They're kind of like the Beatles."

Memphis failed to see the resemblance. They frisked him, and led the way to Raymond Calitri. "Hope you like cricket," one of the Fab Three said. "He's got a game on the telly right about now."

It was baseball. Calitri, priggish and smug, was tuned to the playoffs. A couple of bodyguards loitered nearby.

"Those two are Digger and Butz," Atley let Memphis know on the way in. Then he introduced

Calitri and Memphis. "Raymond Calitri. Memphis Raines."

"I try," Calitri said to Memphis, without a hello, "try to be acclimated. To learn your ways. Appreciate your obsessions. But this baseball. It's so bleeding boring, isn't it? Nothing happens. Nothing at all. What's it all about?"

"It's a game of inches," Memphis said.

"Exactly. And who has time for inches?" Calitri said, and he flicked off the TV.

"Where's Kip?" Memphis said.

Calitri appraised Memphis with a sickly smile. "You were the best, Raines. They say after you left, auto theft in the South Bay went down forty-seven percent. That's impressive."

"Where's my brother?" Memphis asked again.

"Ah! Your brother—Kip." Calitri folded his arms and looked down, lost in thought for a moment. "I'm proud of these," he said softly, walking past Memphis to a display of woodworking projects. "The wagon-wheel planter. The dollhouse. The drop-leaf movable server." He gently touched each item, caressing the exquisitely worked surfaces.

Then he went to a window that looked out on the scrapyard.

"Metal is cold," Calitri pronounced. "Cold and ugly. Wood is warm. *Clean.* Provided by nature. To see a piece of furniture take shape—is like watching a child grow. . . ."

Memphis was unmoved. "I'm sure you're working your way to some kind of point. I'll wait right here."

Calitri blinked and smiled. He went to a desk and removed a manila envelope from the center drawer and handed it to Memphis, who opened it. The envelope contained a single sheet of paper, upon which someone had typed a list of fifty automobiles.

"I need those fifty cars—five-zero—delivered to Long Beach Harbor, Pier Fourteen, by eight A.M., four days from now. I'll pay two hundred thousand dollars."

Memphis tossed the list down onto Calitri's desk. "I'm not interested. I'm just here for my brother."

"Indeed. Young Kip," Calitri said. "Young Kip came to me. Had good street credentials: the brother of the famous Memphis Raines. So two weeks ago, I hired him—and advanced him ten thousand dollars."

"Atley told me. If it's about the advance, I can

understand your anger. The debt has to be settled."
Memphis withdrew a tight stack of bills—ten thousand dollars—and placed it on Calitri's desk. "Ten grand from me to you."

"Were it only that easy," Calitri replied.

Memphis gave him a hard look. "I don't see the complication."

"I have four days to deliver fifty cars," Calitri repeated. "And I have no cars."

"Well, that's another problem," Memphis said.

"It *is* another problem, isn't it?" Calitri said, glaring. "It's about me delivering fifty top-end California cars. Because I said I would. Because if I don't, my South American friend goes elsewhere. He buys them from someone else. And that is a humiliation. Because I'm the jackass who couldn't deliver." Calitri's expression turned fierce. "Am I a jackass? Do I look like a jackass?"

Memphis shrugged. "That's a judgment call I'm not comfortable making. Where—?"

Calitri threw the money in Memphis's face and growled, "I don't get off the *toilet* for ten thousand dollars!"

Atley stooped, wincing from the pain in his leg, and gathered up the bills, whereas Memphis's green eyes stayed fixed on Calitri, cold and furious.

"I'm retired," Memphis said.

"So said Muhammad Ali. Three times," Calitri said.

"Where is my brother?"

Calitri went to a corner, where a tarp covered all but the front of a wooden box like a chest. "I made this, too. My first one. Brass extension handles, not plated. Silk coverings, not rayon, lined with spray green Lorraine crepe."

"Where is my brother?" Memphis repeated.

Calitri pulled the tarp off, revealing a mahogany casket.

"Don't worry," he said quickly. Memphis looked ready to pounce. "He's not in it. But at eight A.M. Friday morning, if that boat sets off without my fifty cars, he will be. Here, let me help you make up your mind." He turned and went to the door into the salvage yard, followed by Digger and Butz. Memphis and Atley went after them.

"It takes eighty thousand pounds of pressure to crush these cars," Calitri told them when they were all outside. It was power he clearly had at his disposal. Down aisles between stacks of flattened vehicles, Memphis followed Calitri and the goons. At one point, Calitri stopped, scooped a handful of steel shavings off the ground, showed Memphis, and explained what they were: "The end product."

He dropped the steel shavings into Memphis's palm and turned away.

Memphis stared at the shavings. "Where is he?"

Finally they arrived at the crusher, waiting momentarily while a forklift rumbled onto the scene. It stopped a few yards away, and Calitri nodded at the driver. He switched on his headlights, illuminating the crusher with the half-flattened Trans Am still in the well, Kip handcuffed in the driver's seat.

"Kip!" Memphis called.

"Who's that?" came Kip's voice from inside the crusher.

"Memphis. You all right?"

Nothing for a few moments. Then Kip told him, "There's things I can't feel right now. Like my feet." Memphis stepped toward Calitri, and Calitri gave a quick nod, ordering the operator to give the ram some juice. It came alive and caved the car a foot more, bending metal, causing Kip to scream, and scaring Memphis off.

"I'm waiting for your decision," Calitri told him.

Memphis turned away, apparently considering the offer, then wheeled around suddenly and threw the steel shavings in Butz's face. The man staggered and Memphis snatched his gun, bringing it under Calitri's chin.

Then Digger drew his gun, making it a stand-off.

"Memphis!" Atley yelled.

Memphis glared. "Back off!"

Calitri eyeballed Memphis's hand holding the gun to his throat and motioned for Digger to stand down. Memphis ferociously backed Calitri to the machine and Digger trained his gun on him, waiting for an opportunity.

"You won't do it," Calitri said to Memphis. "You're a car thief, not a killer."

"*Was* a thief, Calitri. *Was!*" Memphis corrected.

"You don't kill people like me, and you don't take your brother and run, because we'd find him. You don't go to the police because we have friends there, too. You do nothing except deal with me. I don't care how the fifty get onto my ship. I just care that they do. You decide."

They stared hatefully at one another. Then Calitri called Memphis's bluff. He looked to the crusher operator, who hit the power to the machine and took another bite into the Trans Am.

Kip howled, and Calitri was out of it now, letting things happen, wondering what would happen, frankly. He was a firm believer in the Fates—you exercised control where you could, figured the odds, prepared for known contingencies, and set yourself up always, always to have the advantage. But then you had to recognize the fact that—what did that bumper sticker say—*Shit happens*. It certainly did. It was happening right now to young Kip.

Your call, Memphis.

He dropped his gun. Calitri's men rushed him, and Calitri gave the order to stop the crusher. The others hardly noticed. Digger and Butz were preoccupied with punishing Memphis—Digger holding him for Butz, Butz taking his shame for losing his gun out on Memphis, punching him, enjoying the contact.

"Stop," Calitri ordered. "He's no good to me dead." Digger let him go.

Calitri unpocketed a folded square of paper, took it to Memphis, and opened it in front of him. The list of fifty cars. He held it out for Memphis to see, then let it flutter to the ground and walked off, trailed by the bodyguards.

"You gonna let the scumbag dog you out like

that, Ray?" Butz complained. They were on their way back to the woodworking shop now.

"That 'scumbag' is the only one can get those fifty on our timetable," Calitri growled. "But once he does? We'll box his bones."

4

Fifty cars.

Atley dropped Memphis off in front of the small, New England–style, shingle and clapboard guesthouse where Kip Raines lived on a hill overlooking the port. Memphis went up the walk, let himself into the living room, and sat down on the couch. The walls were postered with Kurt Cobain, Kobe Bryant, Pamela Anderson, and a glamour shot of a Lamborghini Espada being used as a sun deck for two nude girls.

Kip was in the kitchen, illuminated by cold light from the open fridge. He was wearing a T-shirt, leopard-skin Speedos, and fur-lined moon boots. He came into the living room carrying two beers.

"I heard you were pumping gas. Someplace up north," he said.

"Something like that," Memphis said.

"You're kind of cultivating a new look."

Memphis considered Kip's outfit but held his

tongue. Then Kip offered him one of the beers, as an eye-opener apparently, since the day was just breaking.

"No thanks."

Kip took a pull from the bottle and went back into the kitchen with the other beer. He started to return it to the fridge, then wrapped it in a paper towel and used it as an ice pack against the bruises on his head. "You want somethin' to eat?" he called.

Memphis was up now, standing in the doorway between the two rooms. "You sure you're okay? Maybe you need a stitch."

"Nah. It's a scratch. Hungry, though." Kip limped to the fridge and peered inside. He put the cold-compress beer inside on a shelf that was bare of anything except more beer and a jar of olives.

"What've you got?" Memphis asked out of curiosity.

"I got olives," Kip said. "You like olives?" He spilled half the jar into a bowl, and they went back into the living room and sat down again. Kip put the olives where they both could reach, then popped one into his mouth and bit it. The juice stung his lip, then he chased it with beer and showed Memphis an appreciative nod.

"So what are you gonna do?" Memphis asked him, serious.

"About what?"

"About what?" He was a little stunned by Kip's reply.

"Calitri just wants to know I'm still on it. He needs reassurance. All these big swinging dicks do. No worries." The car crusher of a few hours ago was now a distant memory. He picked up another olive, but dropped it back into the bowl. His lip was still smarting. He'd forget that, too, in another minute. Memphis stared at him.

"What?" Kip gave him a grin. "Things are cool. I'll deal with Calitri tomorrow. Work a deal—get some kind of extension. This is handled, man."

"Handled?" Memphis was incredulous. "You just got *crushed* in your car. You're *bleeding* all over yourself. . . ."

"Okay, it wasn't the best day," Kip allowed.

Memphis stood up and went to the window. A crane was unloading a container of Hondas—legitimate cars—at the harbor below. "Does Mom know about any of this?"

"Hey, now, this is none of her business," Kip said.

"Other than the fact that she's our mother."

Memphis was restlessly wandering around the room now. He eyed an old baseball trophy of Kip's, then picked it up and looked hard at it. What had happened to Kip in the last six years?

"You know," Memphis said slowly, "I can understand the silence, the unreturned phone calls . . . but what is really confusing me is how, since I've been gone, you went from being *this* guy"—he indicated the trophy—"to a guy with his head all the way up his own ass."

Kip was visibly stung. "Look, this is just a speed bump," he said. "Don't rub my nose in it."

"By the way," Memphis added dryly, "you're getting blood on your olives."

At the docks in San Pedro, Castlebeck and Drycoff were conducting a police interview on the bleached planks of a small commercial wharf. The subject was Fuzzy Frizzel, lowlife and police informant.

"Get off my back," Fuzzy complained. "I told you, I don't know shit about it." He looked around nervously, wishing for a little more privacy. He had his reputation to worry about. "All I know is, two weeks ago an order was put on the street for a lot of top-end cars."

"Who's doing the boosting?" Drycoff needed to know.

"No clue," Fuzzy told him.

Castlebeck looked skeptical.

"I do not fucking know!" Fuzzy insisted. Drycoff detected a trace of earnestness and gave Castlebeck a questioning look.

"Get outta here," Castlebeck said, through with Fuzzy.

They still didn't know who was doing the boosting.

Helen Raines, dressed for work in a pink Quality Cafe uniform and chunky shoes, was clear-eyed and still attractive in her sixties. She carried three plates across her arm to a booth of kids in UCLA shirts and spread them across the table from memory according to their orders.

"Enjoy," she said. Then she turned and noticed a figure in the doorway that gave her heart a pang of joy and a stab of anger and resentment as well.

Randall.

She went to him, tentative, started to hug him but didn't. Instead she ushered him to an empty table by the doors to the kitchen where they could talk. Memphis noticed she was wiping her eyes.

"You're here about Kip, aren't you?" she said when they'd sat down.

"What happened?" Memphis asked her.

"I don't know," she said honestly. "He met some people and he changed. He lost that sweetness. He'd stay out late. Sometimes he wouldn't come home."

"Why didn't you tell me? I would've come back," Memphis said.

"I'm the one who asked you to leave in the first place," she reminded him. "To save *him*. But you were the one who was saved—you got away from here. Away from the life. I was afraid if I told you, you'd come back and it would start all over again." She took a deep breath. "Tell me, how deep in is he?"

"Deep," Memphis told her.

"Can you get him out?"

"It means doing things. Things I swore to you I'd never do again."

Helen looked away. There was a line at the door now; they needed the table.

"Let's get up," she said, and they did. Helen touched his arm. "Do what it takes, Randall," she told him. "Do what it takes to get him out." He nodded and started to go. She stopped him and this time hugged him tight.

Outside the cafe a new Mercedes S500 pulled up in front of the hydrant by the curb. Castlebeck and Drycoff got out and approached Memphis.

He stopped. "The new Mercedes S500? Very nice."

"Hot off the shelf," Castlebeck said, emphasizing the word *hot*.

"Mercedes improve it?" Memphis asked.

"More leg room, nicer stereo," Castlebeck said, beginning to sound like *Consumer Reports*.

Drycoff changed the subject. "When'd you get back?"

"This morning."

"What for?"

"No particular reason," Memphis said. "Catch a Lakers game. I heard we got Shaquille."

Castlebeck's irritation showed. "Tell you a story. This is funny."

"What?"

"I get a call from a uniform cop. Axton. Smart guy. Iron-trap memory. Remembers everything—birthdays, criminal records, faces."

Drycoff nodded. "He's amazing. He even remembers Kajagoogoo."

"You're right, Detective Castlebeck," Memphis said. "That is funny."

"I haven't told you the funny part yet," Castlebeck said. "Axton says, 'Guess who's in town? Randall Raines.' I say, 'Randall Raines, the car thief? Impossible.' And Axton says, 'Hey! I'll bet you two hundred bucks I just saw him!'"

"Wait a minute, Detective," Memphis said.

But Castlebeck kept going. "The irony is, two nights ago, we snared thirteen fresh stolens waiting for export. And I actually thought, 'Hey! This feels like Randall Raines!' It was sloppy, not up to your former flash. But still, it just felt like you. And now—hey, here you *are*."

Drycoff nodded. "It's uncanny."

Memphis gave them a pained expression. "Look. I don't know what you boys are looking for," he said. "I just got back last night. Family emergency."

Castlebeck wouldn't quit. His answer: "Me, too—I gotta go tell the wife I just lost two hundred bucks."

"And she's mean," Drycoff said, playing along.

"Scorpion-mean," Castlebeck said, but he wasn't talking about his wife now. He wasn't playing or kidding or screwing around now. He was threatening.

44

"Six years ago, you made the smart play and retired from a life that was going to get you caught or killed. Not putting you away for the big hit is a bug up the ass of my otherwise distinguished career."

"Without disappointment, you can't appreciate victory," Memphis pointed out.

Castlebeck bristled. "You learn that from Eleanor?"

"That's hitting below the belt," Memphis said.

"Roll through a stop sign, Randall. Jaywalk. Use an aerosol can in a method other than directed on the label. I don't care what it is—you make one slip-up and I'll send you away for a long, long time."

Drycoff added, "By the time you get out, asshole, there won't even be cars. We'll all be cruising around in spaceships."

"Okay, guys," Memphis said. "Have a nice day." And then he disappointed them by walking away instead of getting in a car.

Castlebeck and Drycoff went back to the Mercedes. "Who's Eleanor?" Drycoff asked as he pulled away from the curb. "Girlfriend? Wife?"

"Eleanor?" Castlebeck said, smiling. "A car."

The sign on the door said as much about the owner as the business inside—a business of restoring old cars.

Otto Halliwell himself, in his late sixties, was the grease-soaked one who could be seen examining the four-inch top chop on a 1954 Ford Vic; or managing the blueprinting of a Chevy engine being installed in a 1961 Buick Invicta; or inspecting the welting and top-stitching on new upholstery for a 1947 Chevy convertible; or pinstriping the flame on a 1934 Ford three-window coupe.

Otto's woman, Junie, was the striking one—early forties, body of a thousand dances—who could be seen wiping Otto's brow like a scrub nurse as he worked.

Otto's mutt dog, Hemi, was the roguish one, age indeterminate, who could be seen mangling in his jaws the leather-wrapped, two-hundred-dollar SpeedMart aftermarket steering wheel.

Memphis Raines stood in the doorway, taking it all in.

"Am I dying?" Otto cried when he saw who it was. "Are all the angels of my life returning to bid a final farewell?" He wiped his hands, held Memphis at arm's length, and looked him over. "And have my angels completely lost their fashion sense?"

Memphis smiled, thinking about the signature black leather duster he had long since packed away in a box. "Hello, Otto."

"Randall, Randall, Randall. *Good* to see you." He was serious now. They were family, connected not by blood but by memories of battles they had fought and won together.

"You, too, Otto."

"You remember Junie?"

"Of course." Memphis nodded her way. "Hi, Junie."

"Hello."

How long had it been? Six years? "I got your postcard at Christmas," Otto said, showing him the bulletin board. Up there with the receipts and For Sale notices fringe-cut for removable telephone numbers.

"See how good it goes with the other one you sent me? Six years ago. Two postcards in six years. You lose your pen?"

"You never wrote me," Memphis pointed out.

"No. But once a week, I telepathically send you warm thoughts."

"Those I got," Memphis assured him.

On the wall near the bulletin board, the framed photograph of a car captured his attention. It was a Shelby Mustang GT-500, white with red pinstriping.

Eleanor again.

Otto saw him looking. "You ever catch her?"

Memphis turned away from the picture. "Eleanor? Haven't tried since I left." He surveyed the shop, the stockpile of collector cars, the feast of tools and machinery, the craftsmen at work. "What happened here?"

"Whatever do you mean?" Otto said. As if it had always been this way. But of course, it hadn't. If the walls in Otto's shop could speak, to the police in particular, he and Memphis and several others they knew would not be free men.

"The chop shop," Memphis said. "Where are the stripped cars? The rolled-back odometers? The part bins? What happened?"

"What happened? I'll tell you what happened." Otto removed the ball cap from his head and ran his hand over the thinning hair on top. "Old age happened!"

Both men smiled. Then Otto said, in all honesty, "I tired of killing them. I woke up one morning and thought, 'I am no longer a destroyer. I am a means of resurrection.' Now we restore. We revive. There are so few things in this life we can prevent from decay. Most must die." His eyes went to the cars. "These don't have to."

Memphis knew the feeling. He'd walked on both sides of the tracks—the wrong side in L.B., the right side in Independence. Otto was right. You had a choice. You could destroy, or you could build.

It made him question his motivation for seeing Otto again. Thanks to Kip, Memphis was getting ready for another walk on the wild side, back to the life. Why bring an old friend into it with him? If Otto went to jail now, at sixty-something years of age, he might never come out. Otto had made a beautiful world within these walls—why risk destroying it?

Maybe for the same reason that Memphis was risking everything that he had built. Otto's world here and Memphis's world in Independence were not stand-alone places. They weren't autonomous worlds, unaffected by everything else that was going on around and in between them. They were parts of the bigger world, the imperfect world that included men like Raymond Calitri. That included black markets, vehicle registration blackouts at national borders, corrupt customs officials, greedy politicians, fraudulent parts distributors, chop shops, and boost rings that victimized and wasted impressionable kids like Kip in the name of the almighty dollar. That's why he was here. If he and Otto didn't build in the world, then men like Raymond Calitri would surely have it destroyed.

Otto was speaking to a Mexican man standing at a compressor. "It's three coats of primer and twelve coats of black acrylic lacquer before laying out the flames—and fill the cab top with mylar flakes. They'll sparkle like the stars."

Then he led Memphis to an automotive audio display built into a plywood wall near the door to the office. He punched the play button on a cassette deck, and instantly engine sounds ripped from the shop's stereo speakers. Otto listened as if it were a Mahler symphony.

"The Ferrari 365 GTB/4 Daytona. At Le Mans, 1971. The quad-cam V-12! Hear how they got the engine up? Hear those exhaust notes? That's a very wide rev range. Here, it peaks at fifty-five hundred rpm." They listened for a few seconds more before Otto stopped the tape and invited Memphis into the office.

Otto poured coffee into Styrofoam cups and set them out on the calendar paper blotter on his worn wooden desk. Then the men sat down. Memphis took a sip, Otto looking at him appreciatively. He hated to spoil the mood.

"What do you know about Raymond Calitri?" Memphis asked him.

Otto's expression changed only a little, just enough to give Junie a look. "If you'll excuse us, sweetness," he said. She hesitated. "Go, go . . . we're fine here," he said.

Junie went, and so did Otto's good mood.

"She gets nervous, anyone from the old days comes by," Otto told Memphis, reassuring him that this was nothing personal. His assessment of Raymond Calitri was brief and to the point. "He's a jackal," Otto said. "Tearing at the soft belly of our fair town. He's amplified much sorrow on these streets. And he's an asshole, to boot."

At least they were on the same wavelength. The time to ask for Otto's help was now. But still, he felt strange about it, asking for something so abruptly after so much time apart. There was a long silence between them.

"I heard about Kip," Otto said finally. "Are you considering a comeback tour?"

Otto already knew why he'd come. "Do you think it can be done?" Memphis asked.

"How many cars?" Otto asked the practical question.

"Fifty."

"How many days?"

"Four."

"How many in your crew?"

"One. But right now I'm negotiating for a second—"

"Fifty cars in four days? I'd say no. It can't be done. You need time to prep, time to shop. You'd also have to hope Kip's jerk circus didn't undo Castlebeck's linkage so much that he's setting up surveillance teams on every city block. A job of this magnitude requires a good two weeks. So, no. It can't be done."

"It has to be."

Otto studied him, then nodded. Imperfect world.

"What about the old crew?" Memphis asked.

Otto leaned back in his chair and struck a wistful pose. " 'A people is a detour of nature to get six or seven great men—yes, and then to get around them. . . . ' Nietzsche said that. I don't know where they are, the old crew, our six or seven great men. Since I've cleaned up, they no longer come around. A pity how legitimacy makes you unpopular. Let's make some phone calls." He motioned Memphis to the phone on Junie's desk.

Memphis thought about her and gave Otto an out. "I understand if you don't want to help me with this."

"Look around you," Otto said. "These days? I'm all about second chances." And Otto closed his eyes and punched a button on a tape deck on a shelf behind the desk. The sound of the Ferrari tape came over the bookshelf speakers on either side of the room.

"Ahh. Eight-point-eight to one compression."

6

The Dodge Aries K with the Pleasure Cruise Driving School sign locked its left wheels between the tracks of the double yellow no-passing divider line perfectly in time with the approach of the oncoming pickup, missed it by inches, and caromed off the windbreak onto the shoulder. The timid Japanese girl behind the wheel negotiated the vehicle back onto the macadam in front of a tour bus, which lurched and offered her a long blast of its horn. The certified instructor in the passenger seat, Donny Astricky, was howling. "Pull over! Pull her the hell over!"

The girl turned the Aries onto the shoulder, jerked to a stop, and twisted the key in the wrong direction. Donny Astricky rammed the shifter into park, yanked the keys out of the column, and chucked the ring out the passenger-side window temporarily.

He then proceeded to fill out Jenny's driving

school scorecard, failing her in all categories, then going into more detail at the bottom of the page.

"Can't negotiate turns. Can't signal properly. Can't maintain speed. Can't parallel park. You can't drive. You can't! It's time to acknowledge that and move on. I can't swim. I know I can't. So you know what I do? I stay the fuck outta the pool."

Jenny began to cry, silently at first, then louder, with soft, wet sobs. Donny was confused. On the one hand, he felt morally anguished and repentant—he was supposed to be her *teacher*, after all. Yet she had almost killed him several times that very morning. Thankfully, his cell phone rang.

"Memphis! How ya doing?" Donny said, then listened for about a minute. "When? Sure, man!" He hung up. His spirits were renewed. He looked at Jenny with hope for the future. He grabbed the driving school form he'd just completed, creased it up, jammed it deep in his pocket, got out of the car, and dropped the keys back inside onto the clipboard where it lay on the passenger seat. The top page on the clipboard was a fresh, unblemished scorecard. "The effort is what really counts, Jenny, so I'm giving you a clean slate," he said. "Just go 'round the block a couple times, stay off the Interstates. . . ."

And then Donny ran for his own car as Jenny plowed into a sign.

Drycoff caught up with Castlebeck in the corridor to the GRAB task force offices at HQ. "Those three Mercedes from the boost? All were sold through Dressner Foreign Motors, downtown Newport. All employees clean except one." He handed Castlebeck a rap sheet and mug shot. "James Lakewood. Did a nickel at Folsom for auto insurance fraud."

"Gosh," Castlebeck said. "I bet he neglected to mention that to the Dressner Foreign Motors folks."

Drycoff shrugged. You never knew, right? "He handles all Dressner's lost key orders with Mercedes' German office."

"Let's go to Dressner Foreign Motors and make friends with this . . . James Lakewood."

They found him at the dealership and conducted the interview in the garage, away from the prying eyes of the sales manager. Lakewood paced nervously throughout and chain-smoked.

"This is outrageous," Lakewood told the men.

"I want my lawyer. I'm not saying a word until I get a lawyer."

Castlebeck nodded, loving his job. "That is one option, James."

Drycoff agreed. "And frankly, a reasonable one."

"So call your lawyer," Castlebeck went on. "Tell him you've been arrested on suspicion of grand theft auto. We'll indict you, and he'll bail you out. Oh, I forgot. You'll lose your job. And we'll move on to trial. That okay?"

Lakewood squirmed. "Let's—uh, go over the other option."

Castlebeck laid the offer on the table. "Level with us. Help us. No arrest, no indictment, no bail-out, no loss of employment."

"Okay, okay, okay." Lakewood took a long breath. "I only did it once. Kid came to me. Said he'd pay five hundred dollars a key. I put through the order forms. He picked 'em up a couple days later."

Drycoff: "When?"

Lakewood: "A week and a half ago."

Castlebeck: "Name?"

Lakewood: "We kept it anonymous. No shit, I'll take a lie detector test. Well-built kid. Looks like a boxer. What's the punch line here? What do you want me to do?"

Castlebeck: "When he comes back, call us."

Lakewood: "What says he comes back?"

Castlebeck: "A hunch. I'm a cop. We get those."

Memphis was on the phone, a legal pad before him with a list of names—his old gang. At the top, Donny Astricky was checked. With each rejection, a name was crossed off.

Dan and Mikey were out. They were in Chino, doing a nickel apiece.

Bill Doolin was dead, scragged in Denver.

Henry Santoro's live-in hadn't seen him in the three years since he'd gone to Florida with Frankie Fish. She had a few choice words for Henry. Would Memphis mind passing them on if he found him?

The hands on the wall clock in Otto's office were straight up: noon. After the conversation with Henry's live-in, he crossed the name off and looked at Otto. Two names left. Otto looked uneasy.

"Not them," he said.

"There's no one else," Memphis pleaded.

Otto bit his lower lip as Memphis reached for the phone again. He tapped in the number and listened to it ring.

"City Morgue," came a voice at the other end. A kid. Intern, Memphis guessed. He asked for the Sphinx. A muffled noise on the other end—the kid had his hand over the receiver.

Clunk. Now the receiver was down on the desk. Memphis could hear an argument taking place.

"Just tell him he's got a call," the kid was saying.

"You tell him! You answered the phone!" Another kid. Two interns, neither one of them wanting to relay the message. Memphis grinned at Otto, who couldn't imagine what was going on.

The first intern scowled and went across a tiled floor hallway where a tall, gaunt man was lowering a body into a cool-drawer. The man's ice-blue eyes locked on the intern, who reported meekly, "You got a call." Except it came out like a question, *You got a call?*

Back at Otto's, Memphis heard the sound of slow, steady breathing in the phone. "Sphinx? Is that you?" Memphis said. "Press one if that's you!"

The one tone sounded in Memphis's ear. "It's him," he told Otto, and then he went into his pitch and hoped the Sphinx was listening. He finished and waited until he heard the receiver click back in the cradle.

"Is he in?" Otto asked when Memphis hung up.

Memphis looked thoughtful. "He didn't say—"

Otto's eyes were twinkling. "You've got several Italian cars on the list. Always tricky, always time consuming. So you're gonna need a specialist."

Memphis was afraid of that.

Bacchiochi Foreign Motors sold and serviced imports exclusively—exotics, mostly. The clean, brightly lit service bays with their spotless benches, gleaming wrench sets, and air tools strung over the lifts from spring cords reminded Memphis of a surgical ward.

"Sway, you set up this brake job?" a bulky bear of a man with a three-foot-long graying blond ponytail asked the mechanic on the creeper, half under a Porsche 911.

"He wants the works," the mechanic answered. "Cross-drilled, slotted rotor, 330-

millimeter competition set! The pads, rotors, hubs, and four pots are in the oil wagon!" It was a woman's voice.

"Thanks, Sway," the man replied.

Memphis stepped up and listened. "Sounds like the right side of the engine's running richer than the left," he said.

Sway, under the car, didn't answer—but you could tell Memphis's voice had made an impression by the fully loaded pause that occurred between his comment and when the creeper rolled out, revealing Sara "Sway" Wayland.

She may have been stunned to see him, but she hid it well. "My horoscope said someone from my past was going to reappear," she remarked.

"And?"

"And it was right. The cable guy finally showed up. Now my HBO comes in fine." And she went back under the car.

"Can I talk to you?" Memphis called, leaning over.

The creeper came back out. "Sure."

Something in the way she just waited for him to speak, blue eyes nailing him for the truth and the whole truth, made it extremely difficult for Memphis to find the words that had so easily come out when presenting to the others. "The thing of it is—" he stammered, "I came back because—"

"What time is it?" Sway asked him.

"Five-thirty."

"Shit." She seemed genuinely disappointed that she was going to have to miss whatever it was Memphis was trying to say. "I gotta get out of here. I'm late for work." Memphis reached down a hand to help her up and came back with an oily crankcase gasket. Sway got up on her own.

"You're *at* work," he said. She'd shucked her coveralls and was scrubbing at the sink.

"I got two jobs, Memphis. Working honest is twice as hard."

The other job was at the Nautical Mile Saloon, pouring pitchers to the tough young crowd that came to mill over sawdust and broken beers. Here, the crowd noise, the jukebox, and the highlights show for the Lakers blaring from a half dozen screens all contributed to his difficulty explaining why he'd come.

So he used an old fallback: "You look great."

"Yeah, well, you always were a sucker for flawed existences," Sway said, and moved off.

"Can't we improvise a little here?" he said, following her through the crowd.

"What'd you have in mind?" she called back over her shoulder. "You want to go in the back and get crazy? Better yet, I saw a Cutlass 442 in the parking lot. We can strip down and shine the hood!"

Memphis replied quietly, almost to himself, "No, that's not what I had in mind."

He stopped at a barstool and watched her, pleased that the regular crowd seemed to know her, like her, and greet her when she passed. She went to the jukebox, put on the Beach Boys, then came back to him, put a glass in front of him, and poured a beer into it. Then she looked at him like she had at the garage, only softer, ready to listen.

"Kip's in trouble," Memphis told her, and she frowned.

"What kind of trouble?"

"He took a boost. And he blew it."

She looked at him, getting it. She was a pro. "And you got some Italians—?"

"Six or seven."

"I'm a little rusty," she told him.

"I understand," Memphis said. "And I hated to even come ask you. I've had to ask a few of the others, too. And I feel bad about it. But . . ."

"You have no choice."

"Pretty much."

"Well, I'd like to help Kip, but . . . that was a long time ago. Those days are over for me." And she busied herself with the glassware.

"Okay," Memphis said. "But if you change your mind, we're at Pier Fourteen. It's fifty ladies in twenty-four hours. Two hundred K and Kip's life are on the felt." And he walked out.

The parking lot was on the harbor, where the aromas from the grill were spiked with the pleasantly bitter smells of salt air and brine. Memphis crossed it through round pools of lamplight.

"Raines! Memphis Raines!" someone called.

He turned and faced four men walking their way across the parking lot.

Memphis stopped and asked, "Do I know you?"

"Well, considering the number of times you screwed me out of business in the past—" one of them said.

"I remember you. Johnny B. What can I do for you?"

"Get out of Long Beach. Tonight." A simple request.

"I'll be gone in three days," Memphis promised. "I'm just here on some family business." He wanted nothing to do with Johnny B. He had enough on his mind.

"I know all about your family business," Johnny B. argued. "Word on the street says Raymond Calitri hired you and your brother for a top order—one that should've gone to me."

"That's not the way it happened," Memphis told him. "Look, Johnny—"

But Johnny B. cut him off. "You're leaving Long Beach. Tonight. You can leave conscious. Or unconscious."

Johnny's friends had encircled him now. Memphis complained, "This isn't exactly a fair fight—"

And Johnny B. swung and connected, a glancing blow off Memphis's jaw. He shrugged it off and struck back, his hands lightning. He slugged Johnny in the face two times before the others bore in and pounded him in a huddle, over and over again. Memphis fought back, determined to take them on for as long as he could stand up.

Or at least until help came. Which it did, causing Memphis to suddenly stop fighting and drop his hands to his sides. He looked past his tormentors to the far end of the parking lot. Johnny B.

and his goons were momentarily confused by his passivity.

"Now it's *really* not fair," Memphis said. The others turned and followed his line of sight. Across the parking lot stood the Sphinx, next to a drop-dead gorgeous Hemi Roadrunner. The Sphinx had a Zippo lighter out, showing them, Statue of Liberty–style, how the butane flame resisted the wind. The other demonstration he'd prepared that night had to do with a gasoline-soaked rag he'd used as a replacement part for the Roadrunner's gas cap. The car belonged to Johnny B.

"What the fuck? I remember this freak!" Johnny said, lurching toward him.

The Sphinx lowered the lighter and touched the flame to the rag. He dropped and rolled away as the flame ran up the cloth and found a vapor trail wafting up from the gas tank. The car was automotive history. It blew sky high.

"You *freak*!" Johnny B. screamed at the Sphinx. "You just blew up a classic Roadrunner! You gonna say something before I fuckin' kill you?"

Memphis smiled. "He communicates through his art."

The first two of Johnny's buddies to reach the Sphinx were amazed at how quickly they found themselves feeling broken and tasting asphalt. They must have been tired, and the Sphinx had to be fresh, because he picked up the third thug and hurled him off the dock, a good twenty feet out into the harbor. That left only Johnny B., who lost a shoe in his desperation to leave the scene in a hurry. The Sphinx crouched, picked up the size eleven, flung it hard, and connected with Johnny's ear, forcing him to drop the pass and go down on his face in what could only be described as a self-tackle.

"Nice toss," Memphis said. "Guys at the garage tell ya I was here?"

The Sphinx nodded.

The bar's back door opened and Sway's silhouette appeared framed in a rectangle of light, appraising the situation—the men standing, the men lying down, the barbecued Roadrunner. She rolled her eyes and shut the door on them. Having seen it already so many times before proved that boys would be boys.

"Lookin' good there, Sphinx," Memphis said as they exited the lot. The tall man nodded and very nearly smiled before the two of them disappeared into the night.

———

Otto's back room was set up as the war room, with a conference table and chairs. Memphis sat at the head, attended on either side by Donny Astricky and the Sphinx.

"I just want to thank you both for coming," Memphis said. He knew he was asking them to risk a lot—their jobs, their freedom, and possibly their lives.

"Come on, Memphis," Donny said. "One last walk in the sun with you and the Big O? Sounds real good."

The Sphinx nodded.

"I've prepared a handout," Memphis said, giving them each a list of cars they were expected to steal.

Meanwhile, in the office, Otto had his arms around Junie, whispering in her ear, "So it's okay?"

"I guess it has to be, doesn't it?" she said.

He kissed her and left. She watched him leave for the war room, where she knew Memphis and the others were waiting, depending on him.

When Otto saw the men Memphis had gathered at the table, he chuckled. "Some crew you've assembled," he said.

"How are you, old man?" Donny said, reaching out his hand.

"Donny Astricky. I am a victim of overpowering memories." They shook, then Otto turned to the Sphinx. "Well, well, well! The original crash-test dummy. Hello, Sphinxy, old rum!"

A glimmer of recognition twinkled in the morgue worker's eye.

Memphis said to all of them, "If we put out the word that we're crewing up for a one-time-only job, what you think that'll yield?"

Donny scoffed. "A bunch of strung-out hypes and stick-up men. This ain't like the old days, Memphis. The profession has lost its . . ."

"Dignity," Otto filled in.

"Yeah," Donny said. "*Dignity.*"

"Well, the four of us don't exactly inspire confidence," Memphis admitted.

Donny spotted a familiar make at the bottom of the list. "Wow! They got Eleanor here?"

Memphis looked apprehensive. "I know. Weird, huh?" He'd dreamed about her.

The door opened and one of Otto's employees was there. "Otto, there's someone here to—"

Five men entered the room around him, around his introduction: Tumbler, Mirror Man, the kid Toby, Freb, and Kip.

"Look at Kip," Donny said, genuinely surprised. "All grown up!"

"Hey, Donny," Kip said.

Memphis turned his shopping list over, face down on the table. "What are you doing here?" he said.

"We've come to work it," Kip told him, eyeing his crew, beaming, ready for action.

Memphis shook his head. "That's not happening."

The comment went nowhere, overshadowed by Freb's display of hero-worship as he went to shake the older men's hands, enthralled. "Wow! Memphis Raines. Donny Astricky. Otto Halliwell. And you must be the Sphinx, on account of you never say a word!" He looked around, and Memphis could swear there were tears in his eyes. "All the big names from back in the day!" he gushed. "This is an honor! A genuine honor!"

"Shut up, Freb," Tumbler said, embarrassed for him.

Memphis made a connection with the voice. "Is that little Tommy Tummel? From next door on Pratt Street?" Now he was caught up in it, too. He couldn't help himself. It was like a family reunion, minus the potato salad.

"It is," Tumbler said, pleased to be recognized by The Man. "But they call me Tumbler now."

"Well, that's macho. That's really macho."

Freb had found one more celebrity to idolize.

"This must be Otto's hound, Hemi, who, if the legend is true, once chased a cop car twenty-seven blocks and chewed off its rear fender!" Freb went to pet Hemi. The dog growled and gnashed at the license plate in his paws, and Freb recoiled.

"You can leave now, Kip," Memphis said.

"No, sir, we've got some business to discuss," he said generously. "We've decided to cut you guys in!"

The men at the table shared a look, incredulous.

"We have to protect our interest," Kip continued. "That is, we're a little concerned about what percentage of the two hundred grand you guys are looking for."

Donny gave Memphis an exaggerated drop-jaw look, and Otto began to shake with internal laughter.

Memphis, on the other hand, failed to see the humor in Kip's speech. "Your involvement is through, little brother."

"Is that right? Okay, fine," Kip said. "But you tell me how three washed-up thieves and an old man hope to steal fifty cars in three days. Taking out a few hours for sleep, which you'll need, that's about a car an hour." He shot a glance around the room, checking to see what kind of impression he was making.

"I promised Mom I was getting you out of this," Memphis said quietly. "Which means you're my responsibility."

"I like you—galloping back here after six years to get all Cliff Huxtable on my shit."

"Well, let's just call Mom up right now and tell her exactly what's going on," Memphis shot back.

Kip gave Tumbler an oblique look. "I don't think I want to call my mom right now, do you?"

Tumbler made a show of looking worried. "No way, man. She may *ground* you."

"No TV for a week!" Mirror Man pitched in, trembling, which really cracked them up.

Otto came to Kip's defense then, the older generation sticking up for the young. "I think you have to consider this, Randall."

"His criminal career has officially come to a close," Memphis insisted.

"His life will officially come to a close if we don't pull this off," Otto said practically. "And how do we do that without them?"

Memphis didn't have an answer to that.

"It can't be done and you know it. He got

himself in this hole—let him help to climb out," Otto argued.

Memphis ran the numbers in his head. Fifty cars, three days. Allowing time for sleep, that was approximately one car every sixty minutes. Shop it, case the location, return and boost the car, deliver. Kip was right. It was impossible without them. He turned to his brother and said, "We do this. Then you're finished, okay? Then you're clean. That's the deal."

Kip looked relieved. "You get me outta this," he said, "I'll move to the country. Race go-karts."

Memphis didn't flinch. He was serious about this. "You hear me?"

"I hear ya," Kip said, no joke.

Memphis nodded, but the troubled look on his face stayed. Then he turned to the others with Kip. "You guys have any skills at all?" he asked them.

"Hell, yeah," Kip assured him. "Mirror Man here is our electronics expert. He's got some gadgets you old farts maybe never heard of. Tumbler can drive anything with wheels, and some things without. Toby's a hacker, can do things with a computer that are pretty amazing."

"How old are you, Toby?" Memphis asked.

"Sixteen, but my birthday's in seven months," the boy told him.

Donny said, "What about him?" Meaning Freb.

"Freb can order pizzas like nobody's business," Kip said.

Freb started to protest, tell him his skill, then shrugged. "People gotta eat," he said.

So pizza it was, and true to Freb's calculations, five boxes was just about the right amount for the nine men. Otto wrote the fifty-car list on the war room blackboard while they ate. When they were finished eating, he laid out the plan.

"In order to succeed, you're going to have to go old school," he told them. "One-night boost. Put all your nuts in one basket. And—"

Tumbler choked on his beer. "One night? Are you *crazy?*"

"You got maybe a better plan?" Donny Astricky asked, completely skeptical.

"Yeah!" Kip said. "You spread it out. You move around. Shadow games and shit."

"Right," Memphis said, dismissing the comment. "Go on, Otto."

"Since we're on a truncated timetable, we take a day to shop it, a day to prep, and—"

"Hey," Kip interrupted. "Didn't you hear what I said?"

"Yes. We heard," Memphis said. "Shadow games. But what you have to understand, Kip, is that if you play shadow games, by the next night, the heat is on to you. With a one-night boost, by the time the first cars are reported stolen, your ship's set sail."

Kip and the others nodded begrudgingly. It made sense. Memphis nodded to Otto, who continued his analysis.

"It's a complicated list," he said. "You've got twenty-five that aren't a problem. But then you've got these exotics, tough to find. And these new Mercedes. They require laser-cut keys."

"I got it covered," Tumbler said.

Memphis turned to him. "You got it covered?"

"Covered," Tumbler said.

And Memphis regarded them all, his ragtag band of thieves, his brother's only chance, and for the first time felt like they might surprise him. Felt some hope. "Okay, then," he said. "Let's get to work."

Castlebeck had assembled in the classroom before him every available GRAB task force officer.

"This is what we know," he said. "There's an order on the street for a good many top-end exotics. We busted the first try. That is a good thing. But we're dealing with professionals, and they'll try again, people."

A detective in the front row asked, "Any lead on the boosters?"

"Nada," Castlebeck said. "But our old friend Memphis Raines is back in town. One plus one just might equal two."

Drycoff came into the room in a hurry and reported a break to Castlebeck. "The kid from Dressner Foreign Motors came through. One of the thieves is gonna pick up keys for three more brand new Mercedes Benzes."

The warehouse door rolled up, revealing the massive seaport, the shoreline toothed with a series of wharves. A twenty-three-thousand-ton container ship sat anchored in the harbor beside a giant shoreside gantry crane. This was the holding area for the vehicles. Once they had full inventory, Calitri's crew would load them onto the freighter. Memphis and the others admired the scene from the dock.

An MV Augusta motorcycle rolled onto the planks and came to a stop near them. The rider dismounted and removed her helmet—Sway. The young guys watched her approach with gathering awe.

"Donny Astricky. Sphinx." She greeted them cordially.

"How ya doin', Sway?" Donny said.

"Kip," she said.

"Fellas, this is Sara Wayland," Memphis told Kip's men. "We call her Sway."

The others greeted her and politely refocused on the harbor. Memphis gave her a curious look, and she said, "No questions. I need the dough."

"Then let's begin," Memphis said, delighted to have her on board. He called everyone's attention to the containers stacked before the ships. "False-walled containers, customs-profiled as ball bearings, destined for South America. Four cars per container. That's for later, though. First let's find the ladies on our list, where they live, when they're home, that they're properly insured—and then let's go shopping!"

Calitri's order, or the "shopping list," identified the target cars by make and model. It was Memphis's organization's job now to locate locally owned individuals for the boost. To each of the fifty cars on the blackboard list, Otto ascribed a female code name with magic marker, and it was by these names that the individuals would become known among the thieves.

Toby, smiling, turned from his computer to Memphis. "I hacked into Farmer's Insurance's database and got addresses on Hillary, Natalie, and Tracy."

Memphis checked the board. "Nice work. Those are all exotics."

A few miles from Otto's, the Sphinx was selecting keyed ignitions at an auto parts store with the assistance of a perky salesgirl.

"What model would you like?" she asked him.

The Sphinx stared at her.

"Model x294? Model x293?" The Sphinx shook his head no after each. "Oh, so what you're saying is you'd like the x295!" The Sphinx nodded yes, and they loaded up a shopping bag. "Good choice, sir," the girl said to him on the way out. "Nice talking to you!"

Back at the garage, Memphis and Otto went through the older man's bible, an overstuffed ledger with the addresses of two thousand cars

Otto had collected over years of selling, servicing, and, yes, stealing cars throughout greater Los Angeles. They scanned the book for prospects that were on the shopping list.

Looking sharp in a designer suit, Memphis entered a Ferrari dealership a few blocks off Rodeo Drive. A salesman approached him. "My name is Roger, sir. Can I be of help?"

Memphis let his gaze pin down the salesman. "Roger, I have a problem," he said. "I've been in L.A. three months. I have money. I have taste. I have a duplex in the Marina and a ski lodge in Sun Valley. It's not helping, Roger. Maybe it's because I'm not in the movies, and I'm not a drug dealer, but I'm not on anyone's 'A' list, and Saturday night is the loneliest night of the week."

"A Ferrari will change that, sir," Roger was certain.

Memphis considered. "Perhaps. But you know something?" He indicated the nearest gleaming Ferrari. "I saw three of those outside Starbucks this morning, which tells me one thing. Too many ass-holes in this city with too much money."

The salesman's face fell visibly, but Memphis

held up a finger. "However—if I were driving a 1965 275 GTB?"

"You wouldn't be an asshole, sir," Roger assured him. "You'd be a connoisseur."

"Precisely!" Memphis knew he had Roger where he wanted him. "Doors would open. Velvet ropes would part."

"I don't have one here, but I can get one from the warehouse," said Roger.

"Superb!" Memphis said heartily. "What else do you have in this warehouse?"

At Motor Vehicles a gray-haired registry clerk peered suspiciously over the counter at Donny Astricky.

"I'd like the names and addresses of the owners of these twenty cars, please," he said, and handed her a list of California license plate numbers.

The woman frowned at the page. She gave Donny a sidelong look, then warned him, "It'll take me about fifteen minutes."

Donny smiled. "No big deal. I can wait," he said cheerfully.

She went away, then thought of something else, wheeled around, and came marching back.

"It's two dollars a name," she told him. "Twenty cars comes to forty dollars." A small fortune, apparently.

"That's no problem," Donny said. He thought about the boost money, the two hundred grand.

"We can't take a check without a proper ID," the woman said finally.

"You think of everything. I got cash!" Donny reassured her. Satisfied that everything was in order, she went off and looked up the owners for him.

So far, Castlebeck and Drycoff's only decent lead was the Dressner Foreign Motors key guy, who Drycoff had lately started calling the "Stench Connection," after Lakewood's cheap cologne. Hoping a contact would come for the keys, the two detectives were staked out in a car parked directly across the street from the dealership.

Drycoff noticed how Castlebeck kept checking his watch. "Gotta be somewhere?" he said.

Otto was showing Freb how to disarm a security system by grounding the taillight with a wire to a mini-battery, shorting out the circuit. The alarm system chirped for a second, then died. The door locks popped open, and Otto grinned at Freb, who was blown away to be obtaining a trade skill and the sense of responsibility that came with it.

To Castlebeck, the minutes passed like hours in the stakeout car across from Dressner Foreign Motors. He watched the detail guys soap up the customers and thought about the irony of men attending automobiles they couldn't afford to drive. Not that his role as the guardian of the playthings of the rich and famous was any better, killing time while he *knew* in his heart that Memphis Raines was up to something in this so-called City of Angels.

Castlebeck reminded himself that any day could be "Anything Can Happen Day," and then something happened, sure enough.

Right about dusk, Tumbler pulled up across the street, a big kid in a black T-shirt and blue vest driving a Chevy Nova. He took the customer entrance. To Castlebeck, Tumbler stood out like Beavis and Butt-head at the Miss America Pageant.

"Car thief," Drycoff said. "I can smell it on him from here."

Castlebeck reached for the digital cell phone.

Inside the dealership, Tumbler and James Lakewood were exchanging keys for cash when reception transferred the call to Lakewood's desk.

Lakewood picked up and Castlebeck's voice said, "This the guy, James? Black T-shirt, blue vest?"

"That's affirmative, sir," Lakewood replied.

"When he leaves," Castlebeck said, "call us with the owners' addresses, *capisce*?"

"I'll send those forms right over, sir," Lakewood said, going all out. Castlebeck hung up on him. He put his own receiver down, smiled nervously at Tumbler, and said, going for an Oscar, "Fuckin' boss, always on my case."

Tumbler went out the way he came in, squeezed into the Nova, and sped off. Castlebeck and Drycoff left the stakeout and tailed him into traffic.

At Yashiro's, a Japanese place on Seventh, Mirror Man had scored a pickup job as a valet. He gave a Bentley Azure owner a claim ticket, climbed behind the wheel, and roared off. A block away, he drove into a parking place. From under his jacket, he pulled a small device called a transponder, which he used to copy the code embedded in the key. Finally he opened the glove box, located the registration, unpocketed a mini-recorder, and made a note of the owner's address.

At a shopping center in Bel Air, a four-wheel-drive vehicle with big BAA tires pulled up near an ATM. As soon as the driver got out, Kip rolled forward in a minivan and screened the driver's side from the cash machine. Memphis hopped out and slipped a rubber bladder between the truck's window and the door seal and pumped it up, prying the door away from the glass. Then he inserted a camera scope into the opening, read the key serial number off the lock mechanism underside, and snapped a photo.

By the time the driver returned with his cash, Memphis was back in the minivan with his collected gear. He and Kip watched the truck go; they would see her again soon.

Otto had finished the chart—the fifty cars now had fifty female names. Everyone but Tumbler was there, and they assembled before the board, considering the task ahead.

"Why do you call 'em girls' names?" Freb asked.

"Code," Memphis told him. "You say Jane or Lucy or Shirley lives at such and such address, and no one listening on the waves is the wiser."

Tumbler entered, excited, waving a small envelope with Dressner Foreign Motors printed in the return address corner.

"Got them," he said. He turned the envelope open-end down in his palm, and three bright keys slipped into view, earning him cheers and a few slaps on the back. Then they toasted the day's work with beers.

Outside the warehouse, Castlebeck and Drycoff were in a celebratory mood as well. Tumbler had led them to what Castlebeck was calling "the mother lode." Through binoculars, he was getting a clear view of cars parked in front of Otto's that he knew belonged to some of L.B.'s most notorious thieves. "See those cars?" he said to Drycoff, handing over the binoculars. "You're lookin' at Memphis Raines, Donny Astricky, Otto Halliwell, and even that fuckin' Sphinx freak."

Drycoff took a look. "And the younger generation, too?" he said. "Kip Raines and his people?"

"Yeah. I have to say I'm disappointed in Raines over that," Castlebeck said.

Drycoff put Castlebeck's binoculars back in the glove box. "Do you think it's on tonight?"

"A definite maybe," Castlebeck said. He radioed the dispatcher and connected to GRAB for three surveillance teams at the addresses he'd gleaned from Lakewood. "The targets are Mercedes Benzes, S class, brand spanking new."

To Drycoff he said, "If it turns out tonight's the night, we'll be waiting."

In Beverly Glen, at the first surveillance site, a 1999 CL 500 sat in the driveway of an opulent home. Parked next door was an inconspicuous panel van occupied by three men: a GRAB uniform and two detectives—Castlebeck and Drycoff.

"I became a cop because of *Mannix*," Drycoff said, eternally bored. "I watched a lot of *Mannix* as a kid. Mike Connors running and shooting and falling outta cars."

Castlebeck chuckled. "It was false advertising." He grabbed the radio mike and said, "Unit Two, report."

"No action yet, sir," a voice said back, the transmission crackling a little.

"Unit Three, tell me something," Castlebeck said.

"Sorry, sir," the officer there replied. "No one's showed yet."

Then the officer in front of Castlebeck's own van spoke up. "Sir? We're on."

Castlebeck peered out the window. A minivan had rolled to a stop at the curb in front of the surveillance site. Two men got out and approached the Mercedes. "Well, hello there, Memphis Raines, and you, too, Kip," he said, recognizing them at once, even in the dark.

The uniformed officer was eager to strike, but it was up to Raines to make the first move. "C'mon, she's a sitting duck," he said of the car.

But Memphis only held up a camera and snapped a couple of pictures. Then he and Kip retreated, getting back into the minivan and driving away.

Castlebeck smiled. "Relax, boys. It's not on tonight. He just came for the photos. He's casing the boost. They and the others will show up at the other cars, too, and they'll do the same thing. Sit, watch, make a photo for whoever's doing the boost. I don't know about you, but I'd like to get some sleep. Tomorrow's going to be a long night."

Drycoff agreed. "If they're replacing the order of thirteen cars that we nabbed, it will be a long night. Thirteen boosts in one night? That's tough!"

Castlebeck gave the driver instructions to drive them back to the office. "We'll pay a visit to Otto in the morning," he said. "Kick over a few rocks, see what's under 'em."

Up in the hills, Donny and Freb were camped out in another minivan.

Donny called for everyone's attention on his radio. The rest of the gang was on standby, listening in. "Okay, seventy-three Firebird," he said.

The voice of Memphis came on and replied, "John Wayne in *McQ*?" Matching vehicles and celebrities. It was a trivia game.

"That's being obscure," Donny said. "Who else? Better known. Otto?"

Back at the garage, Otto in a headset gave it his best shot. "Jim Rockford. *The Rockford Files*."

In the parking lot beside Club L.A., Sway and Tumbler pulled up behind a custom, cherry-red

1950 Merc. Tumbler drove, and Sway took the pictures.

"She's here every night," Tumbler told her. "Belongs to the owner." They pulled away, and Sway picked up the CB mike. "Gimme Columbo," she said.

"Peugeot convertible," Kip answered correctly.

The Sphinx and Mirror Man were listening on handhelds as they crossed a warehouse roof. Donny's voice challenged, "What *color* was Columbo's car?"

"Gray." Kip again.

Mirror Man was impressed. He'd seen *Columbo* plenty of times and couldn't say what color car he drove. "How you know that, man?"

"Remember who my brother is?" Kip replied on the air. In the parked minivan, he glanced at Memphis, who was watching a Cadillac Escalade pull up and enter a garage.

"Hey, three words, everybody," Mirror Man said. "Get a life."

Freb's voice came on next. "Okay, what was on Magnum, PI's license plate?" While waiting for an answer, he and Donny recorded a radio-control garage opener electronic code on a Palm Pilot.

"I know," Tumbler came on. " 'Robin 1.' That's what Magnum's plate said."

"Wasn't Robin that faggy guy who hung with him?" Kip said.

Memphis took the mike from his hand and said, "No. That was Higgins."

Donny elaborated from his location, "Jonathan Quayle Higgins, to be exact."

The warehouse rooftop that Mirror Man and the Sphinx were traversing was the Ferrari storage facility that Sway had researched with the unwitting help of one of the dealer's own salesmen. The men stopped at a skylight to get a look at what locks and security cameras they could see inside.

"Anyone?" Otto said. "The significance of 'Robin 1' on Magnum's license plate?" No one replied. "Memphis?"

"Robin was Robin Masters," Memphis said, remembering now. "He owned the estate they lived on."

"Ten points for our fearless leader," Otto said. "Now, Sway, how 'bout giving us the honor of the Bill Bixby trifecta?"

Sway and Tumbler's minivan was still parked at the nightclub, away from the manager's vehicle now. The work was done; now Tumbler was ready to play. He reached over and put his hand on Sway's thigh, and instantly she grabbed his fingers and twisted them. While Tumbler writhed in pain, she answered Otto.

"He drove a Corvette in *The Magician*, a Ford pickup truck in *The Incredible Hulk*, and—" she paused.

Otto allowed, "Here's where it gets tricky."

"In *The Courtship of Eddie's Father*, he walked! Got it!"

Donny said, "Walked like a bastard. Skippin' stones and shit."

Mirror Man said, "Y'all really need to get the fuck out of the house more."

At night, the International Towers Condominiums glowed with lamplight diffused in the huge panes of glass that afforded its residents breathtaking views. Cabbies used it like a lighthouse. At the foot of the tower was a self-service subterranean garage for the exclusive use of the residents. Memphis, Donny, Freb, and Kip were waiting there now for someone to come and open the door. A gleaming Range Rover obliged, leaving by the radio-controlled garage door. Before it completely closed behind the car, the men were under it and inside the garage.

Memphis led as they walked along the rows of parked cars, searching.

"She's been living here for three years now," Memphis told the others. He turned a corner and spotted her. "There she is. Eleanor. The sixty-seven Shelby Mustang GT-500."

Donny filled in the younger men. "Eleanor is Memphis's unicorn."

Freb asked, "What's a unicorn?"

"Fabled creature," Donny explained. "You know. The horse with the horn? Impossible to capture? In this business, it's the one car that, no matter how many times you try to boost her, something happens. You never win."

Memphis walked over to the car and around it, talking softly.

"What's he doing?" Freb whispered.

"He's talking to her," Donny said. "Getting reacquainted. They've had a rough history. Don't worry about it. It's not a problem."

Freb gave Kip a worried look. "It's true," Kip said. "He's out there, man. W-a-a-a-ay out there."

Donny put a hand on the back of Freb's neck. "Not at all. You see, Eleanor almost killed him a few times. He flipped one on the Harbor Freeway."

"Drove one off the Long Beach pier," Kip said, remembering.

"One of 'em blew up," Donny said. "You

really don't want to know the rest. He's just really got a lot on his mind. . . ."

Memphis finished up and returned without looking back. "Let's go."

"See ya tomorrow night, Eleanor," Donny called.

"Yeah, see ya," Kip said. And he walked off, leaving Freb, who shrugged at the car.

"Uh, so long. . . ."

The gang reconnoitered at Otto's before breaking up for the night. Inside the loose circle formed by the three parked minivans, Donny held forth.

"One thing to remember. On boost night? Always take along a good mix tape. You bring Nancy from accounting back to your crib, you don't put on Sly Stone or James Brown, right? You put on Ravel, Rachmaninoff. Same with boostin' cars. You can't steal a Maserati listening to Sinatra. You gotta get *urgent*. You gotta get Sonny Rollins or *Led Zeppelin IV* or that shit. But never, never, ever take no Allman Brothers into a Lincoln Town Car, or it could lead to disaster."

A car pulled into the driveway. It was Atley Jackson. Calitri's man. Memphis wasn't pleased. They knew their job, and even though, technically, both gangs were the means to the same end, participation by Calitri or his people would interfere. "What are you doing here?" Memphis demanded.

"Came on my own," Atley told him. "Calitri doesn't know—he's not very optimistic about this operation. Neither am I."

"Why not?" Memphis asked him.

"Should I be? There's two days left and we haven't seen car one. Not to mention he's looking for any excuse to kill you."

"We're doing this my way, Atley. Tell him not to worry."

"He ain't worrying, Memphis—I am. 'Cause he keeps planing, scraping, and sanding that coffin for Kip."

Memphis looked over to where his younger brother stood by his car. Then he looked at Atley with determination. "My way, Atley."

Memphis and Kip got into Kip's car and pulled away from Otto's, out into the night. At first they did not see the new Mercedes that pulled out behind them and followed.

Kip steered into a tight alley that led toward his house. The Mercedes turned in behind him, and he was instantly alert. "I don't know anyone else who uses this alley much," he said, his eyes narrowing as he looked into his rearview mirror.

Suddenly there were lights in front of them— not slowing but speeding up as they came closer! Kip slammed on the brakes, but both cars kept coming, sandwiching them in between. The Raines brothers knew what was happening. It was a hit! Now that the Mercedes was close enough, Memphis could see Johnny B. and his gang in the car. An assortment of sawed-off shot-guns and assault rifles were aimed in their general direction.

"Get out!" Memphis yelled. "That side!"

Kip didn't need any more encouragement. He shoved open the door before it was too crumpled to move. Memphis slid across the seat, and the two leaped to the top of a Dumpster and over a fence. As they sprinted away, Memphis heard the spray of gunshots from their pursuers.

Three of Johnny B.'s gang jumped from the car and chased after Memphis and Kip on foot. In the meantime, Johnny B. took the others and backed his Mercedes out of the alley.

Kip and Memphis were now running across postage-stamp–sized backyards in their attempt to escape. "We blew up his car!" Memphis explained to Kip, as if that would justify the situation.

"You could have mentioned that!" Kip yelled. "It's nice to know these things."

Before Memphis could reply, they had another fence to jump. They vaulted together, Johnny B.'s goons right on their tail. Memphis landed waist-deep in a children's pool, while Kip landed heavily in a sandbox. Memphis scrambled out of the pool and turned to see a figure coming over the fence. Kip came to the rescue, picking up a Tonka truck and hurling it. It struck Johnny B.'s man right in the forehead, knocking him backward over the fence.

Kip and Memphis raced on while Johnny B. followed the action from the road, keeping the Raines brothers in sight the whole time. He would nail them if they tried to come out that way. Kip and Memphis jumped yet another fence, this time using a handy clothesline pole to aid them. Memphis landed outside a chain-link dog pen, while Kip landed inside.

The first thing Kip noticed was the enormous doghouse. The second thing he noticed was the name on its front: Beast.

He pushed at the steel door to the pen, but it was locked from the other side. "Memphis, pop the lock!" Kip hissed. "There's a dog in here named Beast!"

As Memphis examined the door catch, Kip heard a whimper. He looked down to see a Doberman puppy whining up at him. "Oh, man!" Kip couldn't help chuckling. "So this is Beast! Cute little Beastie!"

Then he heard a growl, and it didn't come from the pup. Emerging from the shadows was the real Beast—about two hundred pounds, vicious, and angry. At that moment, thankfully, Memphis opened the door, and Kip was able to slide out, his heart hammering. As they ran off, Beast slammed against the door, barking furiously.

More fences. But as Memphis began to crest the second one after Beast's yard, he jumped back and yanked Kip down, too. A shotgun blast ripped a hole where he had just been. It wasn't bad enough that they had Johnny B. tailing them—now some lunatic was pumping shots at them for trying to go through his backyard. The only safe haven seemed to be the open back door of the house next to them. Memphis and Kip ran inside. Johnny B.'s boys came behind them.

The three stoners who sat in the living room never even seemed to see them. One of the stoners sucked on an enormous bong as the three watched Kirk and Spock argue on the TV. Only after Memphis and Kip had vaulted over the coffee table toward the front door and Johnny B.'s boys had gone barreling through did one of the stoners think to say something.

"This is good onion dip."

Out in the front yard, Memphis saw the All Stars, a nearby interstate truck stop. A highway patrol car sat in the diner parking lot. "Come on!" he shouted to Kip. "All Stars!"

As they bolted inside, Johnny B. sped into the parking lot, stopping his Mercedes between two big-rig wreckers, tow trucks for eighteen wheelers. "I can wait, Memphis Raines," he muttered, settling in.

Kip and Memphis entered the diner, noticing the two highway patrolmen and the two big-rig wrecker drivers at the counter. Through the window, they could see Johnny B., waiting. "We're gonna be in here all night," Kip whispered.

Memphis whispered back, "As long as they can see me, they'll sit out there. There's a window in the men's room. Here's the plan." He leaned closer, still whispering. When he was done, Kip nodded, then got up and went to the men's room.

Memphis approached one of the big-rig wrecker drivers, who was just getting ready to leave. "Hey, mister! Is that your truck out there?

The big-rig wrecker? It's been a lifelong ambition of mine to operate one of those."

As Memphis distracted the truck driver, Kip shimmied out the tiny window over the stall in the men's room. Once outside, he came around the side of one of the wreckers and unspooled the tow cable. As quietly as he could, he slowly slid under Johnny B.'s Mercedes and hooked the tow cable to the axle. Then he moved to the other wrecker. Johnny B. and his gang watched the diner, oblivious.

Inside, Memphis was finishing up. "Well, thank you very much for the information, uh—Mel was your name? Want a refill on that coffee?"

"No thanks, son, I gotta be getting on," said Mel. With a wave, he headed out to his truck. He got in, started it up, and began pulling out of the parking lot. The tow cable played out behind him.

Now Memphis sprinted across the lot. Johnny B., seeing Memphis flee, gunned his engine and pulled out. The Mercedes stopped violently, its axle cabled to the wrecker still standing in the lot. Then the cable attached to the moving wrecker snapped taut. *Ri-i-i-ip!* The Mercedes was pulled in half. Stunned, Johnny B. sat unmoving in the driver's seat. The rest of his gang were in the back— which was no longer attached to the front.

Memphis and Kip chose that moment to run out of the parking lot at top speed, disappearing. Before Johnny B. or any of his men could think to go after them, the highway patrolmen walked over. "You got licenses for those firearms?"

7 Back at Kip's house, he and Memphis sat at the kitchen table over a supper of Italian takeout. The TV was on and Kip watched while Memphis flipped through pages of an old photo album, looking at shots of them as kids. He stopped at a picture of their dad, Sam Raines, standing before a Cutlass 442, outside the Raines Olds dealership.

"I wonder what things would be like if Dad hadn't died," Memphis said, thinking out loud. "We'd probably be working selling cars together."

Kip ignored him, watching the tube.

"Remember when Dad used to bring a different car home every night from the dealership? You remember that?"

Kip glanced at him and then turned his eyes back to the TV. "I was six," he reminded Memphis.

"You know, besides just being able to talk to him, I think that's what I missed most about Dad. No different cars every night."

Kip got up, completely unmoved. He stopped at the screen door long enough to give Memphis his take on it all: "Ancient history is two things. Ancient and history."

And then he left. The screen door slammed behind him.

Kip stalked out of the house and across the porch, where there was a view of the harbor, the lights flickering.

Memphis joined him at the porch rail, leaned on it. "What's the matter with you?"

Kip glared at him. "What? You expect me to work nine to five? This is all I know. You make me laugh. You sure didn't mind the easy money."

"I didn't do it for the money, Kip," Memphis defended himself. "I did it for the cars."

"Do you really believe that," Kip demanded, "or do you just not remember?"

"You know what I remember?" Memphis gazed out at the view as he spoke. "I remember Corvettes. All sex and attitude, gleaming by the side of the road. Marina blue, sunfire yellow, marlboro maroon . . . just sitting there, waiting—begging—to be plucked. And I'd do it. I'd boost one and just blast to Palm Springs—instantly feeling better about being me. Like I'd become something else. But you know what? Next day, seems like, cops are coming by, I'm getting shot at, two of my friends die, Atley can barely walk. *That's* what I remember. Eventually, it all closes in."

Kip was disgusted. "Don't feel the need to give me any brotherly advice. Frankly, for you to have the audacity to bring Dad up—I don't even know you anymore. You're not my brother. I've got my own family."

Memphis made a fist but checked swinging it. "Well, when you hit the wall, the same thing is gonna happen. You and your 'family' are either going to get shot or get a five-year-jolt at Corcoran, Level Four."

Kip looked bored. "You know, you're a hypocrite. And I ain't riding with you tomorrow night. I ride with Tumbler. Always have. That's not changing."

Memphis could only stare at Kip for a moment. "Fine," he said. "Ride with Tumbler. I don't even know if we're gonna make it tomorrow night. Might both hit the wall—but I'm still gonna lay it on the line for you. Because in some way, I figure I owe you that. If that makes me a hypocrite, then so be it. After that, you don't have to know me anymore."

On that note, he stomped back into the house, and they were through with each other for the night.

The next day at Otto's, the gang trained on a course of practice steering columns and doors that Otto had set up, a kind of Gold's Gym for boosters. Tumbler modified a series of slim jims based on the makes they were after. Donny packed briefcases with the tools: slim jims, gizmos, screwdrivers, ratchets, dent-pullers, and mini-batteries with pointy leads. Mirror Man was showing off a new tool for Otto—a pager-sized device with mechanical and electronic functions. He demonstrated on a locked Mazda with factory security.

"You just stick it in the lock," Mirror Man said, "hit this little button, and *presto*." The car's doors opened while the alarm made a weak chirp and died.

"We're dinosaurs, Donny," Otto said. "Will somebody pull up a tar pit?" Then Otto asked if he could try, like a kid begging for a new toy.

"Knock yourself out," said Mirror Man.

Two surprise visits were in the works for Otto and the gang that morning; two cars were already on the way. One was a brand-new BMW, and the other was a 1989 Cadillac Coupe de Ville.

The BMW was on its way over from the harbor area impound, driven by Detective Castlebeck, who was accompanied by Detective Drycoff. "This is very nice," Drycoff said about the ride. "Very smooth."

Castlebeck looked at him sharply. "Don't get used to it. It's on loan. We gotta return it next week."

The Cadillac, driven by Freb, was a lot closer to Otto's. He announced himself on the intercom so Tumbler would let the garage door up for him, and the other guys would get the full effect of seeing the Cadillac rolling in out of nowhere.

It got their attention, all right. "How 'bout these apples?" Freb said, climbing out from behind the wheel. "I boosted it! You gonna tell me I can't represent on the night?"

The other guys did look slightly impressed.

"How'd you get her?" Donny asked.

Freb's face lost some color at that. "Actually, the keys were in it."

Donny laughed. "Well, now that defies the point, don't it? All right, get the damned thing in here and get it cleaned up."

Freb pulled the car forward and popped the trunk. Kip came over to look.

"This thing's loaded with crap," he said. "Get a duffel." He removed a leather bag of golf clubs and lowered them into the heavy canvas bag Freb had retrieved from the supply cabinets. Then Mirror Man plucked something else from the trunk and said, "Holy shit!"

It was a plastic bag filled with white powder.

"Lemme see that," Donny said. He pierced the skin and tasted.

"Heroin."

"No shit?" Kip said. They pulled back the tarp that was in the trunk and found themselves looking at a couple dozen similar smack-filled bags.

"There's gotta be a million bucks' worth here!" Donny said, dazzled.

Tumbler was overwhelmed. "Goddamn! We're rich!"

Memphis stepped in and the others backed off a step. "Where'd you pick her up, Freb?" he asked.

"In front of one of them poker parlors in Chinatown."

"Think about the person who owns this car," Memphis said. "You ripped him off. I'm sure he's very unhappy with this situation."

"He's got insurance," Freb said.

"On the car, yes. You ever consider why a car

like this in a neighborhood like that would have the keys left inside?"

"No."

"Maybe," Memphis said, "because no one in that neighborhood would be stupid enough to rip it off."

"Good point."

Memphis looked at the plastic bags of smack and thought a minute, then pulled the bag of clubs from the duffel and tossed them in on top. "Take it back."

"Take it back?" Kip said. "What do you mean, take it back? Are you crazy, man?"

"*Take it back*," Memphis said.

Mirror Man tried to smooth things a little, "Hey, now, Memphis, c'mon, man. . . ."

Donny grabbed Mirror Man and made to yank the bag of smack away, but Mirror Man held on. They lugged back and forth until they both lost the bag and it hit the ground and split in a little avalanche behind the car.

"Now see what you did!" Mirror Man said, glaring. He and Donny were close to coming to blows, and Memphis thought for a second he'd have to come between them, but that's when the car honked in the driveway.

The BMW was there.

"Who is it?" Otto called.

"Castlebeck," the visitor replied.

"Jesus!" Donny said. "The whole damn thing's loaded."

"One minute!" Otto said, and they all scrambled to hide the training course, their tools, and the lists of cars.

"Be right there!" Memphis called. He picked up the broken plastic bag, stuck it in the trunk, and slammed the lid. There was still a neat white pile on the floor, but he didn't want to touch it, and there was no time to get a broom and dustpan because Castlebeck and Drycoff were already ambling in.

"Well. Look what we got here. A multi-generational gathering of shady types. Hello, Otto," Castlebeck said.

Otto put on a welcome face. "Detective. Nice to see you."

"It's been a long time," Castlebeck said.

"Yes, yes. You look well."

Castlebeck walked around the garage, taking it all in. He stopped a couple of feet from Memphis and the pile of smack on the floor. "I gotta tell you, Memphis, seeing you here, with Otto and Donny Astricky, it's getting me all kinda nostalgic."

Memphis said, "Me, too. It's like a big old reunion. You should stick around, 'cause a little later, we're gonna make s'mores and sing 'Cumbaya.' "

Castlebeck touched the trunk of the Cadillac. "What's this?" he said.

"Cadillac," Otto answered.

"What's wrong with it?" Castlebeck wondered aloud, walking around it, his polished black shoe barely missing the pile of heroin.

"Needs brightening," Otto told him.

Castlebeck took out a walkie-talkie and called his dispatcher. "Run me down a tag. Three-two-nine-H-R-O. Cadillac."

He put the walkie-talkie back in his inside jacket pocket, opened a door, and stuck his head inside the car. Then he walked around back, rested his fingertips on the trunk, and rocked the suspension a little, watching the other men's faces to see if anything registered or got away.

His foot was a scant inches away from the pile of white dust.

"No faith in our newfound goodness?" Otto said to Castlebeck.

Memphis noticed Tumbler reaching quietly for a length of pipe on a workbench.

"Sure," Castlebeck said. "But sometimes we

got to create some numbers. The task force is run by statistics, you know? Number of arrests, value of stolen property recovered, that kind of thing. Is that Kip Raines there?"

Kip nodded. "How ya doin', Detective?"

"What are you doing these days, kid? You working?"

"This and that. Odd jobs."

"Odd jobs. I like that. It's what we call a *euphemism*."

Kip shrugged. "I don't know nothing about them police codes."

Before Castlebeck could respond, the radio crackled, "There's no want on the license at this time."

Castlebeck looked disappointed. Otto grinned. Castlebeck stared at the Caddy, still unconvinced, then looked over at a workbench and spotted a legal pad. He casually walked over and saw that the top page was a handwritten list of police unit call signs.

Tumbler had a tight fist around the metal pipe now, ignoring Memphis's facial exhortations to back off, and Castlebeck's current position put his head just above the strike zone—a little high and outside, but definitely a good place to hit.

"You're thinking, Detective," Memphis said

Kip (Giovanni Ribisi) liberates a brand-new Porsche from the dealer's showroom.

Atley Jackson (Will Patton) tells Memphis (Nicolas Cage) that Kip is in big trouble.

Tumbler
(Scott Caan)
is all attitude.

Johnny B. (Percy Miller a.k.a. Master P) and his boys deliver
a warning Memphis won't forget.

The Sphinx (Vinnie Jones) announces his presence with a *boom!* as he blows Johnny B.'s car sky-high.

Otto (Robert Duvall) and Memphis make plans as the others look on.

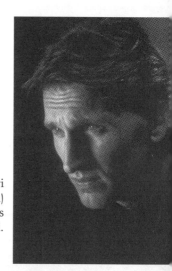

Raymond Calitri
(Christopher Eccleston)
is Long Beach's
crime lord.

Memphis and his gang are ready for action.

Toby (William Lee Scott) and Kip are set for a boost.

Otto marks the blackboard that has
the list of the fifty targeted cars.

Detectives Drycoff (Timothy Olyphant) and Castlebeck (Delroy Lindo) stake out the scene of a possible boost.

Sway (Angelina Jolie) adjusts the rearview as she boosts another of the "ladies" on Calitri's list.

Sway and Memphis wait behind a Lamborghini for the coast to clear.

The infamous Memphis Raines boosts another car.

Driving Eleanor, Memphis eludes the police.

The Sphinx and Donny Astricky (Chi McBride) prepare to ambush Calitri's men at the salvage yard.

loudly, dramatically, "that, okay, there's no want on the vehicle, *but* they probably stripped its guts and crated 'em up, right?"

Castlebeck gave him a long, languid look, then stepped over until he was right in Memphis's face and far from Tumbler. "Something like that."

Castlebeck had stopped his foot inches from the heroin again. Memphis walked around him, opened the driver's-side door, and gestured Castlebeck in.

If Memphis was bluffing, Castlebeck saw no reason not to call. He got behind the wheel—

"Let 'er rip," Memphis said.

Then he turned the key. The engine roared. The blast from the tailpipe dusted the heroin pile clean off the floor, and Memphis winked at Otto.

Castlebeck cut the engine and got out. "Okay then, boys," he said, looking around. Then to Memphis, he said, "Catch you later, Randall."

"Double meaning intended, right?" Otto said.

"Right."

Castlebeck stopped at the gate and turned back to them. "It's funny. There's probably been five more cars stolen in the time I've been here."

"I don't think so, Detective," Memphis said. And Castlebeck was gone.

It took Memphis about two seconds to get in

Tumbler's face. "What were you gonna do?" he yelled.

Tumbler was aback. "I was gonna bonk him."

"He's a *cop*," Memphis said. "What exactly do you think we're doing here?"

"Come on, man," Tumbler said.

Memphis shoved him hard. "I'll say it again. My way, my rules. That's the drill. For the next twenty-four hours, no decisions are made on your own. You got a choice between mustard and mayo on your turkey sandwich, you run it by me. Got it? Everyone? Got it?"

The younger gang members mumbled assent as, to their horror, Otto began dumping heroin from the bags in the trunk into the sink, under a running tap.

"They're on to us," Memphis told them. "If anything appears out of place tonight, not right, cut bait. Walk away. He's sniffing close."

To Freb, he said, "Get rid of that car."

Outside, Castlebeck and Drycoff were pulling away in the BMW.

"It's on for tonight," Castlebeck said.

"How do you know?"

114

"They've got the call signs of our Friday night units on a list inside. Somebody left it out on a workbench."

"Powers of observation."

Back inside, Memphis and Donny were taking the final steps to ready the boost gear. Memphis turned to Donny. "You get gloves for everybody?"

"Yeah." Donny showed him a bag full of gloves.

Tumbler broke into the conversation. "You don't need gloves, man."

Donny was incredulous. "You just gonna leave prints all over these cars?"

"Fire it up, Mirror Man," Tumbler called.

Mirror Man came over with a slim briefcase. Inside were several opaque sheets that contained ten sets of fake fingerprints. Memphis watched in amazement as Mirror Man used tweezers to remove a print from a set marked with Memphis's name. He took Memphis's hand and carefully placed the print over the tip of his index finger, where it stuck, covering the real print.

Memphis and Donny could only stare at the finger.

"How old school do you feel now, boss?" Donny said after a long pause.

"It's worse than that, Donny," Memphis groaned. "I'm afraid we're the school they tore down so they could *build* the old school!"

In accordance with Memphis's instructions, the men left Otto's after that and dispersed until sundown. When they returned, they were dressed for the night: Otto, Donny, Sway, and the Sphinx from Memphis's old crew; and Kip, Mirror Man, Freb, Toby and Otto's woman Junie. They waited anxiously in the dying light for Memphis, then hooted and hollered when he appeared, finally, in his old duds—black turtleneck, boots, pants, and a long, black leather duster.

"That dude," Mirror Man pronounced, "is way too cool for school."

The group assembled before him, and he passed out the developed snaps they had taken the previous night of all fifty cars and their locations, including the Mercedes that Castlebeck and Drycoff had under surveillance.

"We've only got twelve hours, people," he told them. "We know the cops are on alert, but if we keep it real—think slow—we should get through it fine." He glanced over at Donny, who stood by the tape deck. " 'Low Rider,' Donny."

Donny hit the button on the deck, and War's "Low Rider" cranked out. While the younger generation watched in horror, one by one, the older folk started bobbing their heads to the music. Kip and Tumbler exchanged a glance, disbelieving.

After a brief chance to allow everyone to get into the groove, Memphis stood tall. "Okay," he said. "Let's ride."

Castlebeck's GRAB surveillance van pulled into the driveway across the street from the first target Mercedes that Memphis and Kip had cased. Castlebeck checked in on the radio, verifying his presence at the site and ensuring that the other vehicles Tumbler had purchased laser keys for were covered, too. "Units Two and Three, settle in for a long night," he told them.

Thus began the waiting game. Castlebeck settled in the van's high-backed captain's chair and laid out a game of solitaire on the briefcase in his lap. Drycoff turned to the window on the target vehicle, content to simply watch and wait.

Mirror Man and the Sphinx's first target of the night was a Bentley Azure registered to Reverend Lloyd Bidwell, and the boost was an office visit. Junie released the men in front of Bidwell's place of business, beneath a theater marquee that proclaimed in large type, THE LORD GIVETH, AND THE LORD TAKETH AWAY. The old movie poster cases held posters extolling the reverend and listing the hours of services.

Mirror Man found the marquee amusing. "The Lord don't giveth me shit, so I gotta taketh," he explained to the Sphinx. He was discovering another side to the giant—the fact that the Sphinx never spoke made him surprisingly easy to talk to. Mirror Man selected a key from a ring tethered by a chain to his briefcase, compromised the Bentley's driver's-side door lock, leaned in, and sprang the passenger side. Both men climbed in, and the Sphinx inserted his boost tape, a Bavarian polka. Mirror Man was agog.

"Man, you must be deaf *and* dumb," he said, and they pulled away.

Otto released Memphis and Sway at a 1967 Corvette Stingray. Memphis keyed the door, opened the passenger side for Sway, and gadget-

sprang the ignition lock. He put in a Springsteen tape and shot off.

Kip and Tumbler approached a chopped 1950 Merc. Tumbler was going on about Memphis: "Like, it's okay, Memphis was the shit back in the day, but come on, that was then and this is now, and he's all acting like he's The Man, but he ain't The Man. We The Man!"

Through all this Kip was going on about the Merc, how tabloid newspapers spread the car's image as the prototypical mob vehicle, then before you knew it, every pseudo-hood in the fifties started driving 'em chopped. . . .

Tumbler was the first to realize the partners weren't listening to each other. "Yeah, whatever, man," he said. "You're talking pseudo-hoods; I'm talking us."

By now, they were in the car and running. "Same difference," Kip acknowledged, and he inserted his boost tape—Tupac. Common ground. They banged fists and roared off.

Donny and Freb's first girl was a 1999 Infiniti Q45. Donny jimmied the door and they got in, Freb driving. He dead-shorted the alarm system with no problem, but he just could not figure out how to get her started.

"What's the matter?" Donny asked.

"It's all microchips and shit," Freb complained.

Donny unpocketed a low-tech, slotted screwdriver and stabbed it in the crack between the upper and lower dress panels on the steering column. "I don't care what kind of car it is, how fancy, how expensive, how new. You pop the collar, it's 1966 all over again." He cranked the tip along its length, snapping the panels apart, exposing an ordinary ignition.

Freb nodded vigorously. "Cool!" He got it running.

Then Donny popped in his tape. Led Zeppelin blared out, and they hauled.

Half the distance back to Calitri's warehouse on the harbor, Sway stopped the stolen Corvette at the address of a 1956 Thunderbird. Memphis stood up out of the 'Vette and waited for a dog walker to move along before slim-jimming his way in and trouncing the ignition. Fifteen minutes later, he and Sway came roaring onto the dock in both cars, where they were met by five others within seconds of each other.

Otto erased names from the tally board as Atley directed the cars inside the warehouse like a traffic cop. "Right this way, gentlemen," he said, "and lady," when he saw Sway.

Memphis got out, and the others loosely huddled. "Next up, three Mercedes," he told them. He tossed a laser-cut key to Donny, and another to the Sphinx, his old crew. Then everybody got in the vans and broke away for Round Two.

Drycoff spotted them halfway down the street—Memphis with Sway, coming onto the scene in a Volvo, headed for the first staked-out Mercedes. Sway, the driver, banked the Volvo over to the empty curb and let Memphis out. He walked briskly to the car and brought out his laser-cut key. It looked like it was going to be the easiest arrest of Castlebeck's entire career until he saw Memphis stop short for some reason and look at the empty driveway of the house next door.

Where is the van that was parked there last night? Memphis wondered. He turned his head slightly and saw, from the corner of his eye, something like it parked across the street. Stiffening slightly, he pocketed the key and went back toward the Volvo.

Memphis had turned in such a way that no one in the van could see his actions. Castlebeck was practically beside himself. "What are you doing, Memphis?" he said through clenched teeth. "*What are you doing?*"

Sway saw him and backed up to meet him. He got in. "What's wrong?" she asked him.

"Hit it," he ordered. Sway obeyed, pulling out. Memphis continued, "Last night, there was a van parked at the house next door. Now it's at a house across the street."

"You sure?"

From his jacket, Memphis retrieved a photo from the previous night. Behind the car in the picture, a van was definitely parked next door. It definitely looked like the one across the street, too. Memphis glanced into the sideview mirror and noticed the car that was following them. "We've got company," he informed Sway. "Hang a right here." Then he pulled out his cell phone and dialed.

In the car, the driver radioed to Castlebeck. "He's pulling a turn. If he does it again, I'm going to get burned."

"Let's take him," Drycoff suggested to Castle-beck.

"We can't," the frustrated Castlebeck replied. "We've got nothing on him." With a sigh, he said into his radio, "If he turns again, let him go."

Donny Astricky almost jumped out of his skin when the phone went off in his pocket. He was so close to putting the key in the second target Mercedes that he almost decided to unpower the phone instead of take the call. Let 'em leave a message. The problem with that was Memphis had said he wanted the phones on. So Donny knew he either had to answer it, or let it keep on ringing in his pocket. *Okay, fine!* he thought, snatching the little device from his pocket. He answered gutturally. "Yeah?"

"Donny, the Mercedes are dirty. Walk away." It was Memphis's voice in the tiny handset.

Dirty? He and Freb were practically in the car! *Dirty?* Except for eye movement, he froze. There was a van parked down the street, he noticed now. He took a few steps in its direction, away from the driver's-side door of the target, and headed around the car's rear to where his partner was standing. Freb met him halfway.

"What are you doing?" Freb said, completely in the dark.

Donny grabbed a fistful of Freb's shirt in front and pulled him along as he backed up. He was using Freb as a screen.

The GRAB cop watching it happen from the van down the street picked up his mike and reported to Castlebeck. "Captain? Donny's backing off. They've made us."

The bad news came in just after the horrified detectives realized that they had to let Memphis and Sway go.

Castlebeck was beside himself. "Shit!"

"Back! Back, I say!" Toby hollered at Otto's dog. The boy and Otto were trying to have supper. Hemi was going for Toby's french fries, but Toby wasn't sharing. The dog stalked off and finally lay down with a growl.

"Now what, Otto?" the kid said through a mouthful of cheeseburger. "Couple years, we'll all be dinosaurs."

"Makes you think that?" Otto said.

Toby brought three laser-cut Mercedes keys out of his pocket. "Look at these! Encoded laser zaps a code message to a receptor in the engine block!"

Otto was stunned, not by how the keys worked, but by the fact that Toby had them in his pocket. They looked exactly like the keys Memphis was supposed to have in order to boost the Mercedes.

"You want to tell me what you're doin' with those, boy?" Otto said, worried.

"These?" Toby shrugged. "We got these the first time we tried to boost for Calitri. These are to the cars the cops got, remember?"

Otto felt better. "Hung on to the keys, did you? Whatcha going to use 'em for?"

"I don't know. Nothin', I guess," Toby said, dropping them into the paper cup his french fries had come in.

There was a sudden commotion at the door to the garage, and they got up to see who was coming in.

The whole gang was back, agitated and all talking at once.

"Goddamn it. *Goddamn it!*" Memphis shouted, shutting them up.

Otto went to him. "Hey, settle down."

"The Mercedes are dirty. Surveillance vans."

Donny looked disgusted. "He ain't shittin'. It's a hornet's nest."

Memphis turned to Kip. "Where did those laser keys come from? Who did you get them from?"

Kip's eyes went to Tumbler, who said, "The guy at Dressner Foreign Auto, man. Same guy we used before."

"Dressner?" Memphis said. "How long ago was that?"

"Last week," Otto said, according to what Toby had just told him. "Kip's boost."

Donny threw his head back, struck with the realization. "Ah, Christ! Castlebeck got to the guy at the dealership and turned him!"

"Gotta be," Sway said. "It's the only explanation."

Memphis looked at Kip. "You understand what this means? There's eight hours to go!"

Donny lay down on the hood of a 1957 Chevy. "It's over. I ain't going out there again. If we got no Mercedes, there's no reason to boost any of the others."

Kip stood there, speechless, nervous, dumbfounded.

"Memphis? Uh . . ." It was Toby.

"What?" Memphis said rudely. He was upset—
the kid didn't deserve that. The gang tried to make
up for it by giving him their full attention.

"We still have the keys from the first night."

Now everybody looked at Memphis. "Those
Mercedes are in the police impound. You want us
to steal the Mercedes from the police impound?"

"It's worth considering," Otto said.

"In the course of human endeavor, there have
been more difficult things attempted," Donny
pointed out.

It was their only shot. "Okay," Memphis said.
"Where are the other keys?"

Toby led them into the back room and—

"Hemi!" Toby yelled at the dog, who was wolf-
ing the remains of his and Otto's burgers. Desperately Toby's hand swept the scraps of paper food
wrap on the floor into a pile—including a scrap of
waxed paperboard. "He ate the keys!" Toby cried.

"Hemi?" Mirror Man said. "Hemi ate the fucking keys?"

Otto put his hands on his hips. "He usually
goes for the license plates."

The Sphinx fixed his ice-blue eyes on the dog's
belly and withdrew from his coat a ten-inch
straight razor.

"None of that," Otto said, and the Sphinx pocketed the knife.

"We'll need those keys," Memphis said. "Toby, go buy some Ex-Lax and two cans of Alpo. It's our only hope."

8

"Maybe we should give him another box," Toby said. He, Freb, and Hemi were on their third lap around the block, and the dog still hadn't dumped the keys.

"He had two whole boxes of Ex-Lax already," Freb said. He kicked an empty tuna can from under Hemi's nose and pleaded, "C'mon, man! What's your problem? Poop! Poop!"

He looked down the street and noticed a car stopping. "Oh, man," he groaned.

"What?" Toby asked before he saw the three hoods get out of the car. They came closer, surrounding Toby and Freb menacingly.

"Just be cool," Freb whispered, his own heart going a mile a minute. Hemi apparently was not bothered, because he chose that moment to squat and drop a load onto the pavement.

"Hey, little man," one of the hoods said to Freb. "I thought I told you before: This is our turf. So you wanna make a move?"

"No, no, man, we're just passing through," Freb assured him. He waved dismissively. "We don't want anything to do with your turf."

"Why, something wrong with where we live?" the hood sneered.

Freb was getting more nervous. "No, it's just not for us. It's fine for you, being it's your turf and all. . . ." he trailed off lamely.

The hood was not satisfied with that answer. He flipped out a straight razor. "So now you're better than us, eh, *puta*? Maybe I should cut you up!"

At that moment, Toby nudged Freb. "Freb . . ."

Freb looked down and saw that Hemi had finished his business. "Uh, just a second, guys," Freb told the hoods. He bent over and started going through Hemi's deposit to find the keys.

"Aw, man, I'm gonna puke!" said the hood with the razor.

"That is disgusting!" announced one of the others. "You two escape from a mental ward or something?"

The three hoods decided that Freb and Toby weren't worth harassing and moved away. As they walked off, Freb heard one of them say, "What kind of pervert gets his jollies playing with dog shit?"

But Freb didn't care what the hoods thought.

He had found what he was searching for. "Got 'em!" he said to Toby, ecstatic.

"All three? Let's go clean 'em up!"

The police impound lot was surrounded by a chain-link fence topped with barbed wire. Surveillance cameras swept the area. The lone security guard in the front office thought that the area was well protected. He only occasionally looked up from his crossword puzzle, roast beef sandwich, and coffee to scan the monitors that displayed any activity in the lot behind him.

Suddenly, the door opened. In walked a nightmare in the form of Mirror Man.

He was in a lather. "Every time!" he said to the surprised guard. "Every time I park my Volvo in Beverly Hills, they tow it!"

"Can I help you?" asked the guard.

"Can you help me?" Mirror Man looked as if the idea were ridiculous. "I don't know. Can you right more than two hundred years of oppression, outrage, and indecency?" He was on a roll. "Can you erase a collective memory of pain and suffering? Can you beat back The Man so's he can't beat back us?"

The guard stared at him blankly.

"Doing your little puzzle there, huh?" Mirror Man slashed an accusatory finger toward the crossword. "How about a twelve-letter word for what I'm thinking? *Motherf—*"

Outside the rearmost section of fence surrounding the impound lot, Memphis stood with Sway and the Sphinx. He brandished a pair of huge bolt cutters, with which he proceeded to cut the connectors binding the fence to its support posts.

Back in the office, Mirror Man continued his harangue. "A brother in a Volvo—it makes folks nervous! Well, that is *wrong*! It's beyond wrong. It's barbaric!"

The security guard tried to get a word in. "We ain't got no Volvos here—"

Mirror Man glanced at the impound lot monitors. Memphis was clearly visible, cutting the fence. The security guard was about to follow his gaze to the monitors when Mirror Man cut in again. "This is where they tell me to go. This is where I picked it up the other four times when they towed me, when all I wanted from Beverly Hills was a decent place for Chinese food. And you say it ain't here? Why don't you just tell me to go out into the yard and sing 'Swing Low, Sweet Chariot'?"

The security guard was astounded when Mirror Man actually began to sing. He desperately whipped open a drawer, looking for a file—any file—on a Volvo.

As Mirror Man sang, he watched the monitors. Memphis finished cutting, and Sway kicked the section of fence aside. Swiftly, she, Memphis, and the Sphinx entered the lot, searching for the cars they wanted. The security guard still had his face buried in his files, but Mirror Man was coming to the end of "Swing Low, Sweet Chariot."

As the song finished, the guard gasped, "Thank God!"

"You find my Volvo?" Mirror Man asked.

"Not yet," the guard confessed.

So Mirror Man broke into a rousing rendition of "Camptown Races."

Memphis, Sway, and the Sphinx located the three Mercedes, fired them up, and drove them out through the gap in the fence. Only when Mirror Man saw the cars whisk out of range of the security cameras did he stop singing.

"Tell you what," he said to the guard. "You find that Volvo, you keep it. Give it to your girlie. Tell her about the life lesson you learned today. About the kindness of strangers. Peace and chicken grease, my friend."

With that, he left the lot, and the puzzled security guard went back to his crossword and sandwich—once again without looking at the monitors.

Up the road a bit, Mirror Man was walking along when a car pulled up. It was the Sphinx. Mirror Man hopped in, and they drove off.

Shortly afterward, at the impound, cops scrambled to the sound of klaxons. Drycoff pulled the surveillance van just in time for the aftermath. When Castlebeck discovered the Mercedes had been stolen, he said, "This means war."

9

After liberating the Mercedes from the impound, the gang returned to the streets.

Donny Astricky and Freb got better acquainted while picking up an Aston Martin DB7.

"It's Freb with a 'b,' right? Where's that come from?" Donny asked conversationally while removing the car's ignition lock cylinder. Freb squirmed, piquing Donny's interest.

"C'mon, you can tell me," Donny said. "We're partners here." He tucked the car's original parts under the driver's seat and replaced them with a new, aftermarket rig with a bright silver key already in the slot.

"My real name's Fred. You know, Frederick? Except one night I got drunk, and I decided to give myself a tattoo. Hot needle it. I used a mirror to guide me."

Freb pulled up his sleeve, and under the dome

light, Donny Astricky could see the results: *F-r-e-b* across his left biceps.

"The mirror messed me up with the 'b' and the 'd,' okay? Everything's reversed in a mirror, you know? Now I'm Freb."

The new ignition was in. Donny gave the key a half twist and *voom*—it cranked.

"Glad to know you, Freberick," Donny said, and they roared off.

In the huge metal Ferrari warehouse, a skylight imploded and glass cascaded onto the concrete floor, tripping an alarm; the Sphinx and Mirror Man had arrived. They entered the building through the broken skylight, dropped to a girder, tightrope-walked it to an iron post, and slid down the post as if it were a fire pole to floor level. They followed the sound of the alarm to a wall-mounted metal cabinet, where Mirror Man first tried a center punch and mallet before shifting the attack to the recessed lock.

"This is made of some state-of-the-art shit," he told the Sphinx, complaining about the hardness of the metal. "But the drill will snap the sockets, which will force back the spindle and release the lock." When the door gave, they toggled off the alarm and went to raise the loading dock's overhead doors.

Memphis, Sway, Kip, and Tumbler were waiting outside. "How's it going?" Memphis said.

Mirror Man smiled. "It's going fine." He jerked a thumb at the Sphinx. "The Quiet Riot and me are swapping trade secrets."

They entered the warehouse as if it were the tomb of Tutankhamen, hushed and expectant. Their flashlight beams danced over row after row of gleaming cars. According to Sway's notes, every model Ferrari they needed was here, mixed among the Daytonas, the Boxers, and the Dinos: a 1987 Testarossa, a 1995 335B, a 1967 265 GTB4, a 1999 550 Maranello, and a 1997 355 F1. Seeing so many amazing cars in one place had the gang awestruck—silent.

"Show time," said Kip in a low voice.

Sway headed for a car. While Memphis and the others waited, she went down the shopping list like a jeweler, cracking the ignitions.

The signature throaty roar of a Testarossa broke the silence, and another Ferrari, and another. One by one, Sway got the cars started and turned them over to the team. Then, like a squadron of fighter planes, they left the hangar and rocketed down the runway of Long Beach Boulevard.

The Ferraris were at Calitri's dockside warehouse with Donny and Freb's Aston Martin and a 1998 Viper that Kip and Tumbler had boosted. The Viper's robotic voice was a nuisance to Atley as he tried to load it into a container—repetitively warning, "You are too close to the vehicle! You are too close to the vehicle!"

The next car on Memphis and Sway's list was a 1971 Plymouth Hemi Barracuda. Sway remembered it from the case as a car usually fitted with a Club, the iron-pipe security bar that wrapped up the steering wheel. "You bring a hacksaw?" she asked Memphis.

"No, open her."

She pulled the window, got in on the passenger side, gizmoed the ignition, and had the car running with the Club still on. Memphis got in the driver's side with a small aftermarket steering wheel.

"Little trick I picked up at the car thief retirement home," he explained.

Sway was impressed. It was a lot easier than sawing. "Very creative."

He popped four rivets on the steering column with a screwdriver and yanked the wheel off with the Club still on it, then centered the new steering wheel and jerry-banged the rivets.

Finishing up in under a minute, he said, "Let's cruise."

Sway heaved the old steering wheel out the window and they took off down the street. They had to turn, and a caution light caught them. Sway came to a full stop behind the white line, not looking for trouble.

"This had to be a chick car," Sway concluded.

The light changed and she went on. "Show you." From the console, she produced a tube of lipstick. Then she dropped the visor, which had a mirror, and wiped some color on her bottom lip.

"Lipstick?" Memphis chortled. "What next? Blush? I like it. You look beautiful."

Sway dropped the tube back into the console and focused on the road ahead.

"Did I say something wrong?" Memphis asked her.

"Fine," she told him. "I'm fine. I was just playing."

Memphis shrugged. "You say 'You look pretty' to a pretty girl and you get scowled at. You seem like a girl from a James Bond movie. I like that kind. In wet suits."

Sway gave him a bored look. The lipstick was on a little thick, but it was oddly effective. Out the window she said, "Oh, wet suits and pink underwear."

"I like pink underwear," Memphis said with a smile.

10

Junie, in a van, was on the cell phone, placing an order for a limo. "Yes, you'll need to pick them up at the Riviera Building, 2206 Beacon Street, Palos Verdes."

A few minutes later, a 1999 Rolls-Royce stretch limo pulled to the curb. The driver got out and entered the lobby of the posh apartment building. Out of the shadows across the street came Kip and Tumbler. They climbed in and drove away.

Detective Drycoff led Fuzzy Frizzel through a dim, steamy locker room in the police precinct. The lowlife informant was clearly spooked at being alone in the locker room with only Drycoff and Castlebeck.

"You were supposed to call," Drycoff reminded him. "It really was a pain in the ass having to track you down, Fuzzy."

"What are we doing down here?" Fuzzy asked nervously.

Drycoff shoved him into a shower stall area. "It's a good place to talk. A little more privacy. And—it's quieter, don't you think?" The question was directed at Castlebeck.

"No comparison," Castlebeck replied. "It gets so noisy up there at times, you just want to scream."

"But of course, you can't," said Drycoff.

Castlebeck looked grimly at Fuzzy. "Down here, no one would hear you. . . ."

Fuzzy's eyes searched frantically for a way out of his predicament. "You're not going anywhere until you've told us everything you know, Fuzzy," Drycoff said.

"I've already told you everything," Fuzzy whined.

Castlebeck wasn't buying it. "Detective Drycoff, is the suspect resisting arrest?"

"Why, yes, Detective Castlebeck. I believe he is." The threat in the words was obvious.

"Okay, okay." Fuzzy rolled his eyes. "Word says Kip Raines took the job—screwed it up royally."

"Really?" said Castlebeck. "Who placed the order, Fuzzy?"

"If I talk, he'll find out," Fuzzy said, panicked. "You have no idea what he'll do to me!"

"You've got no idea what we'll do to you if you don't," Castlebeck said.

Fuzzy gave up. Only divine intervention could help him now. "It's Raymond Calitri's order," he said quietly.

Castlebeck and Drycoff shared a meaningful look. They were finally getting very close.

In another world, practically, an image of the moon floated on a wall of plate glass that fronted a beach house living room. The reflected light infused the moist air over the driveway, giving the appearance of a veil, or thin cloud, blanketing the silver, wedge-shaped 1994 Lamborghini Diablo that rested there.

Like a predatory sea animal, the stolen Hemi 'Cuda rolled to a stop in the shadow by the curb.

"Hello, Tracy," Memphis said, calling the Lamborghini by her code name.

He and Sway approached her together. They were halfway there when a bank of ceiling lights flared in the house and ran them off the driveway into the bordering hedges. As if on a stage, a man appeared in the window, and then a woman, and even from where Memphis and Sway watched them from the drive, it was clear that there were loving looks between them.

"We might be here awhile," Sway said, cueing, it seemed, the couple they were observing into a long embrace.

"So," Sway asked Memphis, "you seeing anybody?"

"No," he told her, keeping his eyes on the window. "I had a girl once. She was great. Problem is, great girls come along once every ten years. So I gotta wait another three years before I'll even bother to look."

"Seven years," Sway said. "Has it been that long? Tell me, this girl was so great, why'd you leave her?"

"It was suggested to me by her parole officer."

She didn't answer, and Memphis turned to look, expectantly. Over her shoulder he saw the 'Cuda's dome light on. One of them had left a door ajar. Seeing Memphis spooked, Sway turned and saw it, too, and then both of them were running for it, chancing it.

They piled into the car and pulled the doors after them, restoring the cover of darkness. For a minute, neither of them said anything. Then Memphis felt around the dome for the switch and broke the circuit there. The couple at the window hadn't noticed, apparently.

Memphis wanted to go back to what they'd started in the driveway. "I asked you to come with me."

Sway thought about that a minute. "You asked me to be a different person."

" 'Cause you would have had to give up the life?"

"I was eighteen years old, Memphis. I was still jacking the rush. You made the decision for all of us."

"Well, you're straight now."

"Yeah. It was different after you were gone. But even straight, I'll never be the kind of girl you—oh, listen, what does it matter now?"

The couple in the window cavorted, on a somewhat different plane.

"I did ask you to come with me," Memphis reminded her.

"And I asked you to stay. But I guess love only takes you so far."

In the GRAB task force office, Castlebeck and Drycoff were reading papers from a thick police file.

"Raymond Vincent Calitri," said Drycoff. "Did

ten years in South London for manslaughter. Immigrated in ninety-one."

"Calitri's into loan-sharking, extortion, fencing," added Castlebeck. "It makes sense that he'd move into car thieving. His front is a salvage yard on the water."

Suddenly, a fist slammed down on the file and yanked it away. "Back the hell off, Castlebeck," a voice growled. The hand continued on, plucking away the papers from Castlebeck and Drycoff.

"Give me those!" said Drycoff.

"Shove it, kid!" said Detective Mayhew from Homicide, now clutching the file. "That's a *Homicide* file from a *homicide* investigation. It took us three months to get a magistrate to give us a wiretap on him. No other department can go near his person, residence, or place of business. Raymond Calitri's going down for murder one, boneheads! Who cares about grand theft auto?"

Mayhew walked off with the files, leaving the other two to meander dejectedly back to Castlebeck's desk. "Nothing like departmental cooperation," mumbled Castlebeck bitterly. He sat heavily, rubbing his temples.

Then he noticed the forensics report on his

desk—accompanied by a plastic bag of glass shards and two fluorescent light bulbs.

" 'Detective Castlebeck,' " he read aloud, " 'the glass shards from the warehouse are from a black-light bulb, available at any local hardware store.' " He thought for a second. "What's a blacklight doing in a warehouse in Long Bea—?"

In an instant, Castlebeck was up and moving back down the corridor. "Come on!" he called to Drycoff.

"Where?"

"A hunch. We're cops, Drycoff. We get those."

He sure goes on long enough," Sway said about the guy in the window, about his technique. Then she turned to Memphis and asked, "What do you find more exciting? Making love or stealing cars?"

Memphis considered the question. "What about making love *while* you steal cars?"

"Good line. But not a lot of girls you can use it on."

"That was a question for you. You didn't answer the question."

Sway nodded. "Sounds dangerous. The—uh,

the—" She moved her leg, straddling the shifter. "The shifter might get in the way."

Memphis moved for her, whispered in her ear, "I want to break in . . . break into your master cylinder . . . use a double overhead camshaft. . . ."

"No, I can't," she said. "Can't have this . . ."

"Ahh," Memphis said, playful. "Straight in-line six. Triple Weber carburetors. Steel tubular frames bolted to each other's body structures . . ." And he kissed her. At first she resisted, but eventually she responded.

They finally broke away.

"Whoa! Good brakes, too!" Memphis said.

"Except that now I've been chopped up, and my parts are in a Honda Prelude being driven to church in South America by some Bolivian consul's wife . . ."

"Leave Bolivia out of this," Memphis said.

"It's time to work," Sway reminded him. She cast an eye at the beach house window—empty, the couple gone. Memphis nodded. They got out of the car and went to the Lamborghini. Sway found the passenger-side door open, let Memphis in the driver's side. Neither of them pulled the doors all the way closed as Memphis unlocked the parking brake and steered the car along a rolling path down the driveway and into the street in the direction of the 'Cuda. Sway stepped out as the car began to pick up speed and hopped into the 'Cuda.

Five minutes later, both cars were growling, tearing north for the harbor.

11

"Freb, this here is Laura. Laura, I'd like ya to meet Freberick." Donny was taking a 1999 Jaguar XJR through the boost process.

"You ever feel bad about any of this?" Freb asked.

"Hell, no," Donny said. "I'm Robin Hood! I take from the rich and give to the needy."

"You mean the poor."

"No. The needy. We need this car!"

Donny pressed the clutch and put her in gear; she was ready to start. Something cold pushed into his temple. He recognized the feeling—it was a gun. On the other end of it was a car jacker, face full of pimples.

"Out of the car, bitch, or I blow your fucking head off!" the little demon whined.

Donny was dumbfounded. "Are you kidding me?"

"Donny, wait," Freb said, eyeing the gun.

"Donny don't wait for shit, Freb!" he said. He threw open the door, catching the kid in the crotch, doubling him over and causing him to lose the gun. Donny stood up out of the car and picked the weapon up.

"You lazy, disrespectin', half-assed bully. Don't you know that any asshole can pull a gun?"

And Donny booted the kid's behind, once, twice. "You don't know how to boost, so you take the damn car when there's a frickin' *person* in it?" Then Donny turned to Freb, still in the car. "I ask you, Freb, what's the matter with kids today?

"Get up!" Donny ordered, pitching the kid's gun in the storm drain. This freed his hands to open-palm bitch-slap the kid over the curb, backward across the sidewalk, and against a wall, leaving him stunned in a heap.

Donny got back in the Jag, gave Freb a bug-eyed, tongue-out, willy-nilly grin, and then peeled off, cackling at the moon, while Jimi Hendrix's "Crosstown Traffic" wailed from the speakers.

Castlebeck and Drycoff were back at the warehouse, where they'd nearly made the nab the previous week.

"Where's all the coffee cups and beer bottles and cigarette butts?" Castlebeck complained. "This is a crime scene. I thought we had it sealed."

"That stuff's over there," Drycoff said, aiming a flashlight at a littered area. A blackboard leaned against the wall.

"Take the blacklight over there," he said.

"You gonna tell me what the hell this is all about?" Drycoff said, plugging a caged safety lamp with a long cord into a wall outlet.

Castlebeck toed the shards of glass still on the floor from the time before. "Remember the seventies? The Bee Gees? 'Stayin' Alive'? Blacklights were all the rage."

Drycoff shook his head. "I'm too young." He handed the lamp over to Castlebeck.

"Okay, they make felt markers with special ink that only shows up under blacklight. You with me?" He clicked the light on and shined it on Drycoff's jacket. Flecks of dust on his lapels picked up the rays and lit up like tiny fireflies. "Now say you had a shopping list of cars you were going to boost. You'd be using the list at night. But you wouldn't want anybody to see it during the day. . . ."

Castlebeck walked the lamp over to the board

on the wall, totally convinced, held the light to it, and there they were—fifty names. Fifty cars.

A few of them were crossed out—the detectives recognized them as the vehicles they had recovered. Some of the others were smeared, erased at the time of the raid. But much of the board was still legible under the blacklight.

"Here's our list," Castlebeck said.

"That's a big list," Drycoff said. "We can't handle all these cars."

"Maybe we don't have to. Let's just concentrate on the rarest, and hope for some luck. Get some guys on the Lamborghinis. You and I will take the 1967 Mustang. Eleanor. She's the jackpot."

"How do you know they haven't already stolen it?"

"I know Memphis. He'll leave her for last."

"Why's that?"

" 'Cause she scares him. Now let's get some names and addresses on the vehicles. Let's go!"

The narrow spiral parking garage was designed for maximum capacity in a minimal architectural space. It was eleven levels of parking in a tower shaped like a corkscrew. Mirror Man and the

Sphinx hiked almost all the way to the top before they found what they were looking for.

"Gina!" Mirror Man said. "Oh, baby!" They moved for her, a two-door Humvee, then suddenly Mirror Man grabbed the Sphinx. "Check it!" he said, pointing to the license plate. It said SNAKE.

"Oooooh! Snake!" Mirror Man said, playing scared. "How much you want to bet that Snake is one bad dude? Don't want you callin' him the name his momma gave him! Uh-uh! Homeboy say you call him Snake!" And Mirror Man cracked up. Even the Sphinx registered a grin as he slim-jimmed her. They climbed in, the Sphinx the jockey this time, Mirror Man the copilot. "Say good-bye to your ride, Snake!"

Outside, near the entrance to the tower, an unmarked GRAB sedan pulled up and idled while the cop inside made a radio call: "We're at the Harbor Towers. We're going in now to check out that second Humvee."

The car was winding down the third level turn when Mirror Man popped in his tape, Albert King's "Drivin' Wheel."

"That's what I'm talkin' about!" Mirror Man screamed. "Drivin' wheel! Drivin' whe-e-e-el!"

They wound around the driveway to the second level, and suddenly Mirror Man screamed for real—a bloodcurdling, consummate scream of horror that welled up from the molecular level and blew out his throat like a siren. This was no tribute to Albert King—it was the primal response to a boa suddenly in Mirror Man's lap, eight feet long, scales shimmering on coiled muscle, slithering up his chest.

The scream caught the attention of the GRAB officer at the entrance. He spotted the Humvee coming down and gunned his car toward the exit ramp to cut it off.

Mirror Man screamed again, a shrill, piercing shriek. The Sphinx swerved wildly into the last turn and met the GRAB car coming head on. The cop slammed on his brakes. The Humvee roared forward, pushing the GRAB vehicle in front of it. The Sphinx was determined to get out of the garage.

"What do I do? What do I do? *He's gonna swallow my shit whole!*" Mirror Man bellowed, wholly concentrating on the boa. *"Hospital! Take me to a hospital!"*

The Sphinx shook his head.

"C'mon, you creepy motherfucker! Take me to a hospital! What are you doing? I'm gonna die!" The boa was around his neck now.

One hand on the wheel, the Sphinx leaned over and pinched the snake behind the back of the head.

Mirror Man shook uncontrollably, crying and fully expecting to die. "You tryin' to make him more mad?" he sobbed.

Under the Sphinx's hand, the snake relaxed its grip. The Sphinx heaved it out the window. Mirror Man collapsed against the door. He did not notice the GRAB car driver's miscalculation ahead of them at the exit. The sedan, in reverse, went over a retaining wall and plowed backwards into a barrier. At the exit, the Sphinx calmly took a pass card from on top of the sun visor and used it to open the bar blocking the way. Mirror Man stared at the Sphinx. Finally, he said hoarsely, "I never thought it'd be possible, *but your ass just got spookier!*"

The Humvee accelerated into the night.

Kip and Tumbler came to Otto at the door to the garage.

"We're done, boss," Kip said.

"Not so fast," Otto said. "There's one more for you—Carol. Cadillac Escalade lives in the suburbs. Junie's waitin' for you in the van."

The young men turned and headed for the parking area. Over his shoulder, Kip heard Otto calling Toby. "One more name to scratch off the list, Toby! Hey, Toby! Where are you?"

Toby was in the van.

Junie never saw him get in, and Kip and Tumbler had no idea he was there, in the little cargo space between the backseat and the rear doors. He rode all the way to the job site. As a matter of fact, they were out of the van before they discovered him at all, when Toby came tumbling out.

"What are you doing here, assface?" Tumbler said.

"I never been to the suburbs," Toby said, grinning.

It was too late to do anything but drag him along. "Just stay behind us," Kip said, "and keep your mouth shut."

A neighborhood security car glided by.

"Look at that," Tumbler said. "People got their own palace guard."

The Cadillac Escalade was in a garage. Kip used a controller that had a recorded remote code, and the door opened. He could hear the sounds of music, laughter, and splashing in the back—a pool party. Clearly, the folks were out of town.

Inside the garage were jet skis, mountain bikes, and other expensive toys. Kip, Tumbler, and Toby took it all in with equal parts fascination, loathing, and envy.

Toby stepped up to the car. "I got this one," he said.

Kip grabbed him and pulled him away before his slim jim could slide into the door. "You open that door, and you'll wake the entire neighborhood!" he hissed in a whisper. "Ever hear of alarms? Go keep a lookout at the back door."

Toby proceeded to the door as Kip searched a Palm Pilot for the proper code to open the car. When he got to the door, Toby suddenly found himself face to face with a beautiful girl about his age in a wet swimsuit. They stared at each other, dumbstruck—two kids from opposite sides of the track. Then the girl moved off, headed back to the party.

Toby went back to Kip. "Come on, man. Let's go!"

"One second," Kip said. "Okay, we're in!" He pressed a button on his Palm Pilot, and the car opened. Toby and Kip got into the front, Kip driving. In another few seconds, he got the engine started. He slammed Carol into reverse and peeled out of the garage just as the girl Toby had met came back with two of her friends.

"Somebody call security!" she yelled as Kip spun a half donut in the street—a big black letter C—threw it into gear, and roared off.

Kip knew there was going to be a pursuit. Add to this the fact that they were in the suburbs, where streets were not laid out in grids, but according to topographical features—to follow an elevation line along a ridge, to avoid a stream or ravine, to keep to the property line of a tract acquired from a subdivided farm. They were as lost as DeSoto bushwhacking for the Pacific.

"Which way's out, man?" Toby complained.

"Shit all looks the same here," Tumbler said.

They did find it eventually, accidentally. It had to be a major route because the neighborhood cops were there—two cars blocking the road and men with their guns drawn.

"Run it!" Tumbler yelled.

"Shit!" Kip floored it straight for the middle, hoping it was something like bowling a seven-ten split, where he knew he'd probably only hit one. The cops had time for a few shots, and one wild, over-the-shoulder throwaway got lucky, drilled the windshield, and came to rest in Toby's shoulder.

The Cadillac swerved onto the grass median, through a road sign, and back onto the road on the other side. Kip punched the gas, getting them out of there.

"Just hold on, Toby," Kip said, seeing his shirt and the spreading stain of blood. "Please. Just hold on."

12

Memphis, Sway, Freb, Mirror Man, and the Sphinx were all back at the warehouse, where most of the cars had been delivered. Atley Jackson already had containers loading onto the cargo ship. Memphis was just waiting for Kip.

"You sure they were waiting for you?" Memphis asked.

"No doubt about it," Mirror Man said.

"It's six fifty-five," said Atley. "We're running out of time."

Kip drove the Caddy all the way in from the boondocks and across Long Beach without attracting a single cop. A stolen car dented along one side with a bullet hole in the windshield and a serious bleeder in the backseat—it was comparable to trolling a slaughtered cow across L.A. Harbor without attracting sharks.

At least the tags were up to date.

"This does not look good," Atley said.

Memphis went to Kip and Tumbler as they moved Toby out of the backseat in his blood-soaked shirt. At least the kid was moaning—not dead yet.

"You're gonna be okay, kid," Atley said. "It ain't as bad as it looks."

Memphis grabbed Kip. "What happened? What did you do?"

Kip's face was ashen. "He stowed away in the van!"

"We didn't know he was there," Tumbler chimed in.

"We've got to get him to a hospital," Memphis exclaimed.

Atley's was the voice of reason. "There's a *bullet* in his shoulder, not a fishhook." He pulled Memphis aside. "Gunshot wounds have to be reported. You can't take him to the hospital. I know a doctor in town with a private practice—emphasis on *private*."

Memphis was worried. "Can he deal with it?"

Atley nodded.

"Okay. Let's move him."

The two of them and Kip moved Toby slowly

to the van. Kip slid in next to him. "I'm going with him!" he said defiantly to Memphis.

"No, you're not," said Memphis. "You're going back to Otto's to wait there for me."

Kip just sat there, not budging.

From the driver's seat, Atley said, "I'll take care of him, Memphis. Go. Finish this thing."

Memphis hesitated, then nodded. Atley threw the van into gear, and it screeched off across the wharf. Memphis stared after it as Sway came over beside him.

"What's the count?" he asked her.

"Forty-nine down, one to go." Sway raised her eyebrow. "The Shelby, Memphis. Eleanor."

"They're gonna be waiting for me," Memphis said. "You want to run interference?"

Sway was already moving toward a van. "Thought you'd never ask."

13

"International Towers. Five-two-three Long Beach Boulevard."

The address was coming in over the radio from the task force office. Castlebeck repeated it and wrote it down in his notebook. Drycoff turned the car that way.

"Now put me through to dispatch," Castlebeck said into the mike. "I need backup."

To Drycoff, he said, "We've got him now. There are only two Shelby Mustangs registered in Long Beach, and one of them is out of town at a car show. It's been a long night, Drycoff, but the sun is coming up now, and I feel like it's going to be a beautiful day in L.A. Don't you agree?"

"You okay?" Sway said.

Memphis nodded and swallowed hard. According to Kip, ancient history was only two things: ancient and history. If that was true, then why was it closing in on him now, pressing him to the wall?

His history with Eleanor was a repeating history. She'd nearly killed him several times. He was on the way to meet her now.

His history with Sway seemed to be just that—history. But the feelings were still there.

"You should know that walking away from this town was hard," he told her. "Walking away from you nearly killed me."

Sway took his hand, squeezed it. "Good luck."

Memphis got out of the van and headed for the underground parking garage that served the residents of Harbor Towers. Eleanor was parked in the same space. Waiting for him.

Memphis walked up to the car and touched the hood lightly, just his fingertips. "I know we got a history together, Eleanor, and that history hasn't been great. But I promise: You take care of me, I'll take care of you."

Memphis went around to the driver's-side door, slim-jimmed and hot-wired her, and in the space of sixty seconds they were gone, breaking the surface, waiting for the light.

It changed almost immediately as Castlebeck and Drycoff pulled up to the same intersection. The Mustang barreled across in front of them.

"Shit!" Drycoff yelled, pounding the steering wheel. "He's out of the bag!" Shifting lanes without fanfare, he closed the distance between them.

"We can do this the easy way or the hard way," Castlebeck said.

Memphis turned onto General K Way and merged into the early morning traffic. By that time, he had seen the unmarked car in the rearview—it was just a matter of time and traffic before he made his break. When the opening came, he released the clutch and went a gear lower for power. But he waited before he engaged it so the Mustang would slow in front of the detectives just a bit, forcing Drycoff to use the brakes. Then *wham!* He popped the clutch and pulled a quick U-turn, sending the detectives a message written in smog and tire smoke.

"I think he's choosing the hard way!" Drycoff commented, preparing to chase him. Just then, Sway's van made a sharp turn and cut off Drycoff, preventing him from going after the Shelby for a few seconds. As Memphis pulled farther away, Castlebeck lost his patience. He grabbed the radio. "This is one-Baker-eleven, requesting backup units!"

Drycoff stuck a bubble flasher to the roof and hit the siren, stopping traffic and hauling it over so he could advance after the Mustang.

In the van, Sway smiled as she drove away from the scene. "I always was a sucker for flawed existences."

"He's getting off," Castlebeck warned, and Drycoff found a way over to the right-hand lane. Memphis was leading them up Lebanon Alley, a tiny, one-way street in the downtown banking area. Castlebeck and Drycoff stayed on Eleanor like a hound.

"One-Baker-eleven, in pursuit," Castlebeck radioed, then gave his location. The dispatch opened a channel and identified the subject's car, plate number, and location: 1967 Mustang, California two-seven-four-Lincoln-Young-Nora, east-bound on Fourth Street.

Memphis squeezed in front of a delivery van, then streaked across Wilshire, dodging the two-way traffic, and reentered the last leg of Lebanon Alley going the wrong way. The reaction from the oncoming traffic was loud and predictable—although when did leaning on the horn ever fix anything?—and Memphis gutterballed out of the way and hung a left.

Two LAPD cruisers converged on him at the next intersection, forcing him to detour into a narrow alley, then back out when a garbage truck

entered ahead of him from a parking garage.
Speeding in reverse for the cross street, using the
rearview mirror as a guide, he spotted Castlebeck
and Drycoff's unmarked car turning in, followed
by a cruiser. It looked like they had him boxed.

Memphis cranked the wheel around, turning
Eleanor into the alley entrance to a parking garage,
then straightened out and floorboarded the car
backwards through the garage. Castlebeck and
Drycoff screeched in after her. Memphis hung
onto the seat back with his right and steered with
his left, backwards, over his shoulder, the length of
the garage. He barely missed a Volvo coming out of
a space.

"Don't worry, honey," he said to Eleanor, "just
pretend we're backing outta the driveway." They
made it out going the wrong way through the time-
ticket dispenser and carved into traffic, still going
in reverse. The kid in the backseat of a station
wagon in the next lane waved, and a Humvee bore
down on him, closing the gap between their hoods.
Memphis could hear sirens coming somewhere
behind it.

Memphis stopped, threw it into first, and
veered over the double yellow line into the lane
that went back. At least it oriented Eleanor in the
right direction. Good thing, because momentarily

a cruiser came on and crossed the center line to block him. He veered right into a parking lot. The police cruiser turned in, too.

Drycoff was also back in the chase, approaching from Main Street.

Side by side, the Mustang and the LAPD cruiser streaked out of the parking lot into Vincent Court Alley—four lanes lined with parked vehicles.

After crossing Seventh Street, Memphis knew, the alley narrowed to one lane. He surged ahead of the cruiser, blew through the cross street, and squeezed in alone—*wham!* Behind him, the pursuit was rammed by a bus, which came to rest across the alley entrance.

Drycoff skidded to a stop short of the intersection and the wreckage.

"That's it! Out!" Castlebeck ordered. "I'm driving."

Drycoff's jaw dropped. Because of the wreck? "That wasn't my fault!"

"Tell it to the judge," Castlebeck said, getting out.

The detectives switched places. Castlebeck tore out of there behind the wheel.

On the outskirts of town, Santa Fe Avenue had light traffic, and Eleanor was clocking eighty miles an hour with no police in the rearview. Then a chopper scraped overhead.

"Sixty-seven Mustang, silver in yellow, single occupant, California tag two-seven-four-Lincoln-Young-Nora," went the dispatcher's call to the pilot.

"I've got him. Heading north on Spring Street." The chopper swooped down.

Eleanor crossed a bridge and disappeared from the chopper's view under a triple overpass, but an LAPD cruiser met her coming in the opposite direction. Memphis spun her 180 degrees and headed back for the overpasses. Another cruiser that had pursued him on Santa Fe arrived, and Memphis turned again onto San Fernando.

Two more cruisers appeared fifty yards ahead of him. One cut off the access to a freeway on-ramp, and the other braked across both lanes of San Fernando.

The streets were now closed. Even if Eleanor could fly, the chopper controlled the sky.

The only thing left was the river.

Memphis guided the car off the roadway into a concrete channel wet with water spewing from an overflow pipe from the L.A. River Basin. Like a log in a flume, Eleanor raced for the sea. Police in the three cruisers waded their tires in after her.

Memphis reached for the dash, yanked the red nitrous oxide knob, supercharging the mixture in the carb, and floored it, leaving the LAPD cruisers sloshing in his wake.

The chopper, on the other hand, continued to skim along, shadowing him, closing in.

"She's in view! Heading south, past Sixth Street!" the pilot reported. Long Beach was crawling with cruisers and unmarked cars now.

"Copy that, stay with him," Castlebeck said.

Memphis shifted into high gear, and the speedometer needle raked through the 120s. He was pulling away from the chopper.

"The suspect is pulling away. I can't keep up with him!" the pilot reported.

"What do you mean, you can't keep up with him?" the dispatch barked.

"He's doing one-thirty," the pilot yelled back. "Gimme an Apache attack chopper and I will!"

"Requesting additional LAPD, CHP, and air support," went the dispatch.

When Eleanor hit 150 miles an hour, the chopper became a nonissue. "He's gone," the pilot said.

"You did it, honey!" Memphis hollered when he saw that Eleanor had dusted the chopper.

"Goddamn it!" Castlebeck yelled in the car. "Where can he exit the basin?"

Drycoff puzzled over it a few seconds. "How about where the seven-ten meets the one-oh-five?" Castlebeck jerked a hard right and raced up an on-ramp to the freeway.

"Suspect is believed to have exited the L.A. River Basin," said the dispatcher.

Castlebeck veered off the next exit.

"Suspect is not in visual, repeat, no visual on suspect," came the news.

Kip and Atley were in the waiting room of a Long Beach clinic.

"What time is it?" Kip asked.

Atley looked at him doubtfully. "It's seven-thirty. Aw, man, I think I better get you out of town. Your brother's the best boost in the world, but I don't know if he's going to make this one."

"I'm not running out like my brother did," Kip said flatly. "I don't just abandon my friends."

"I ought to slap you silly," Atley said. "You think Memphis ran? You better get your story straight."

"Go on, straighten it," Kip said.

"Maybe you should talk to your mother. She

told Memphis to go. She knew if Memphis stayed, you would have walked his line. You would have joined his crew. So she told him to pick up and go. And he did. Thinking it was best—for you. He just left all of us—for you. I guess it wasn't that big of a sacrifice for him, leaving everything behind. And now, six years later, ain't life grand? You ended up a boost anyway."

The "private" doctor came over to Atley. "I sedated him," he said, referring to Toby. "He's sleeping. And Atley—this is the last time. Me and you—we're even."

Atley nodded, satisfied. "Thanks, Doc." He looked at Kip. "See that? Sacrifices."

Traffic was jammed at the eastbound toll plaza to the Vincent Thomas Bridge, cars idling while police worked to clear an accident on the bridge side of the toll booths.

Memphis appeared, bringing the speeding Mustang and a half dozen cop-driven pursuit cars into the mix.

He hit the brakes and skidded to a stop a hundred yards from the bottleneck. The marked cruisers caught up immediately and came to a stop behind him, waiting for Castlebeck to arrive on the scene.

Memphis made a call from the car.

"Otto."

"Memphis?" the older man said. He and the gang were back at the shop, tuned to the police scanner. "Where the hell are you?"

"Leading the police parade."

"I hate to bring this up," Otto said, "but it's seven fifty-one, and you have an appointment with destiny."

Castlebeck pulled up behind the stopped cruisers. He and Drycoff got out with guns drawn. More than a dozen uniformed officers joined them, pacing toward the Mustang. Memphis watched them advance.

"I might be late," he told Otto.

"That's not good," Otto radioed back. "How is Eleanor?"

"She's wonderful. In the pink." He watched a tow truck pull one of the wrecks from the pileup to a flatbed truck. A loading ramp came down off the tail, making an on-ramp. "But something tells me that's about to change. . . ."

He pulled the nitrous oxide knob on the dash, slammed the car into gear, and punched the gas.

The wheels spun, grabbed under the smoke, Memphis zeroed in on the flatbed's ramp, and—

He took it flat out.

He raced up it like he was jumping a mogul, like Evel Knievel, tracking up the ramp and sailing *over* the truck bed, the tractor, the toll booth, the accident scene, and down two hundred feet away.

Slam! The car hit the tarmac and went screaming out of control, swinging wide, toward a concrete barrier, until—

The rubber bit, the car lurched, and Memphis cranked the wheel hard around, sweeping around the barrier.

"Man, can he drive," Drycoff said, and Castlebeck scowled.

"What?" Drycoff said. "All I said was—"

Free at last, Eleanor took off like a rocket down the runway of open road.

14

Calitri looked up from his reflection in the deep finish of the mahogany casket at a clock on the wall.

"Where do we stand?" said Tami, closely examining her own reflection in a hubcap of chrome propped on a shelf of repair manuals outside Calitri's door. Somehow the stroke of cherry color that waxed and traced the edges of her lips had blurred in one of the outside turns around the bottom. With the point of her right pinkie, she adeptly sculpted it back.

"Forty-nine in, one to go," said one of the British boys.

"It's almost eight o'clock," Tami said. "What then?"

Atley and Kip were at Otto's when the minute hand made its final lurch into the new hour. Like a preset alarm in Atley's pocket, the phone went off. It was Calitri.

"Where's Memphis?" he asked.

"Not here."

"Time's expired. We have forty-nine cars. That's one less than required. Bring the kid and we'll settle this. Bring him to my office. I don't want to be anywhere near those docks."

"What kid do you mean?" Atley asked him.

"The kid who won the golden ticket and got to go to the chocolate factory and meet Mr. Willy Wonka," Calitri sneered. *"What bloody kid do you think I mean?"*

"Kip Raines?"

"Right!"

"I don't know where he is," Atley said.

"Tell me, Atley—in America, what do they call a fellow with *two* bum legs?"

"Sir."

"Find him, Atley!"

"What if I can't?" he asked coolly.

"Then big brother takes the fall for the slip-up. Doesn't matter much to me. One Raines is as good as another," he said, and hung up.

Atley clicked off and Kip said, "Thanks."

"Thank Memphis," Atley said. "He just took your place under the guillotine."

————

Pier Fourteen looked deserted. The gangplanks were rolled up, the containers loaded.

Memphis idled Eleanor in the driveway outside the loading docks, where a Calitri man came and said, "Sorry, mate. We're all done here."

"We're not done," Memphis said. "This car is number fifty."

"You're late. Shove off. You got a problem, take it up with Calitri."

To which Memphis turned and slowly motored away.

The man on the platform said into a walkie-talkie, "He's on his way."

"Where's Raymond Calitri's place?" Castlebeck said.

"Exeter Salvage and Steel," Drycoff replied as they sat at the roadblock. "On the water. Why, are we going? Homicide said not to interfere. . . . ."

"To hell with Homicide," Castlebeck grated. And they left for the party.

Memphis was just arriving. He pulled the battered Eleanor, dented and smoking, into the gravel lot. Calitri stepped outside to meet him.

"You're late," he said.

"We're gonna argue over twelve minutes?" Memphis said.

Calitri's eyes stayed cold, looking at Eleanor. "I said fifty cars. Not forty-nine and a half."

Memphis put his hands on his hips. "Pull those dents out, a little fiberglass . . ." He kicked a tire lightly, bent over, looked at the way it barely cleared the fender, and said, "Okay, could use new shocks. Can we make a deal?"

"Offer me something," Calitri said.

"The book on her is sixty, maybe seventy, eighty grand. Subtract eighty from the two hundred you owe, and we'll call it square."

"Done."

Memphis's eyebrows went up. "Okay. Good. And this thing with my brother is over."

"Over," Calitri said. Behind his back, he was slipping his fingers through the rings of a set of brass knuckles.

"Done. Finished."

"Done and finished," Calitri said. Then he wheeled around, full force, slamming a fist into Memphis and knocking him flat. "But not with you. I said eight o'clock, and you're late. I said fifty cars, and you bring me a bloody *wreck*. And you insult me in my place of business."

He turned to a couple of young Englishmen. "Put a bullet in his ear and shred him," he ordered. "And put the car in the crusher."

They dragged Memphis away.

Calitri looked after them momentarily. When they were gone, he went to a wooden cabinet built against a wall, withdrew a bottle of scotch, and poured himself a drink, neat.

"I love this country," he said.

The young Englishmen took Memphis outside, across an open area, into a yard with heavy machinery—a shredder, a crusher, and a tall crane. Off the crane hung a mechanical pincer claw.

Memphis watched the claw drop from the sky and land, open-mouthed, on Eleanor's back. He watched as the jaws closed and held her, then raised her.

"What say we let you watch the crusher first?" one of the Englishmen said to Memphis. "You'd like that, wouldn't you? Watch your little effing car get smashed?"

"Watch now, die later," the other one said.

"Did you want to get shot in the head or the chest?"

"You get to choose," the first one stressed, feeling generous.

"Chest," Memphis said, wanting only to shut them up. Then the man kicked him hard—a cruel, violent strike to the shins, like knocking the foundation out from under him, dropping him shoulder-first to the floor.

Then they looked up at Eleanor. She was swaying over the conveyor belt that led to the crusher and its large hydraulic ram. "She looks a bit like a toy," one of the bodyguards commented. The crane lowered her to the belt and released her there.

If there were scraps after the crush—loose pieces of fender, mirrors, trim—they would go into the shredder, a cutting-wheel machine that could render flat steel to ribbons. Along with Memphis.

"Hey! Fellas!" A new voice entered the equation.

Atley.

What are you doing here? Memphis thought.

Calitri's bodyguards stared.

"Change of plans!" Atley said. "Don't worry—Calitri's coming! Gonna tell ya all about it!"

Atley had seen Eleanor the minute he'd pulled his Cadillac into Exeter—hanging high above the rooftops like a trophy in the jaws of the crane. Three men had come with him in the car—Kip, the Sphinx, and Donny. They'd turned the car in Eleanor's direction and come over right away. But they'd split up into two groups for the attack.

Atley was his own group, charged with creating a diversion, distracting the thugs, whereas the main thrust of the others was toward the machinery.

"Stay right there, Atley," one of the Englishmen said, raising his gun.

"Don't move," the other one said.

Atley didn't have to.

As soon as the claw had released Eleanor onto the conveyor, Kip and the others had stormed the operator behind the scenes. Then Atley had come on, creating his diversion. Now Kip had the claw moving steadily toward the other men. It was coming along like a wrecking ball. When it finally arrived, it hit like a runaway pickup truck and flattened the men to the floor.

Memphis struggled to his feet, spotted Kip, and hobbled to the crusher conveyor's kill switch, stopping Eleanor. Then he turned to Atley.

"Weren't you supposed to get Kip out of town?" he yelled.

"Kip's doin' okay!" Atley said. "Look at him."

Memphis's brother had Calitri's crane operator hogtied on the ground. "I got the Sphinx, Donny Astricky, the whole crew!"

"Then get him out!" Memphis insisted and stalked off.

"Where ya' goin'?" Atley cried, hurrying after him.

"To talk with my employer!" Memphis said. "Stay here. You'll just slow me down!"

While Memphis was on his way to Calitri's office, Castlebeck and Drycoff were arriving at Exeter's front gate. "I'd like to speak to Raymond Calitri," Castlebeck told the guard, showing him his badge.

"Let me call him," the guard said. He picked up a phone in the guard shack and started to dial.

Before it rang on Calitri's desk, Memphis stormed in and punched Calitri in the face. "Let's go over our contract again," he growled.

Calitri was momentarily shocked into silence.

"I boost half the exotics in Long Beach in one night and you want to put a bullet in my head?" Memphis said.

Calitri glared. "Do you know who you're dealing with?"

"Yes—a guy who made the mistake of picking a kid to do his dirty work. Who made a bigger mistake picking my kid brother. Who made the biggest mistake—trying to kill me!"

Calitri grabbed a sharp, pointed, wood-turning awl. He stabbed at Memphis, who picked up one of Calitri's custom wood chairs to fend off the blow.

"Hey, be careful with that!" Calitri admonished, his concern for the chair completely over-shadowing his concern for his own safety.

"Oh, that's right," Memphis said sarcastically, "you have a thing about wood." Calitri slashed at Memphis, but Memphis used the chair to trap his assailant's arm. Now with all the leverage, Memphis was able to slam Calitri into a rack of tools. "Warm. Clean. Provided by nature . . . It's also strong," he continued, swinging the chair and swiping the awl from Calitri's hand. "It hurts," he added, bringing the chair around and knocking Calitri back through the open door to his office. The chair broke. "And yet, it feels good," Memphis finally said, brandishing the remains of the chair like a bat. "Kind of like baseball."

Calitri had made it to his desk now, and from there he pulled out a gun. Memphis threw another chair at him, but Calitri ducked, and the chair flew over him to smash into the glass divider behind him. Calitri came up firing.

Memphis ran from the office, dodging shots,

and Calitri chased after him. "I'm sort of warming up to metal," Calitri said as he lifted the gun again.

"Four-thirteen," Castlebeck radioed from his car when he heard the shots. "In progress. Long Beach Harbor, Pier Fourteen. Requesting backup." Then both detectives left their cars, guns drawn.

Now there were four of them in the game, stalking one another, hunters and prey. In the plant's labyrinthine interior, through a maze of steel girders and pipe, Memphis scrambled for cover, pursued by Calitri, who fired wildly at shadows. The bullets ricocheted off the scrap iron like pinball shots. Suddenly Memphis found himself at a dead end. The only way out was a narrow staircase leading to the plant's upper levels. Memphis scrambled upward. He heard Calitri in pursuit.

Above the bins, scrap racks, and processing machinery that comprised the plant, a grid of catwalks hung, giving Exeter's men a better view of the inventory on the floor, as well as access to the ductwork, electrical systems, and building superstructure for maintenance. It was to these narrow, intersecting footbridges that Memphis led Calitri.

Clearly, Calitri thought he had the upper hand. He started talking to Memphis as he closed in. "Maybe we should recolonize your bloody country! Make the place a penal colony like Australia. We could rename it! Something more fitting. The United States of Rubbish! The United States of Mediocrity! The United States of Weak, Self-indulgent, Crass Sods Who Eat Too Much Fast Food!"

Castlebeck motioned Drycoff to go toward Calitri's office, while he headed in the direction of the gunshots. He entered a long, narrow corridor, then had to climb several flights of stairs.

Moving toward an exit, Memphis saw a shadow between him and the door. He backed up, turned to run, then stopped in his tracks. Across the walkway in front of him was Calitri, who raised the gun and fired.

Memphis recoiled instantly, sidestepped a loose flooring grate, then fell through another. The grate fell four stories, crashing below with a horrendous noise. Dangling, with his fingers clinging to the lip of the hole, Memphis could see Calitri approaching. He struggled to get his leg around a pipe so he could lift himself out. He tried to move quietly—it was evident that Calitri did not see him yet.

Then Memphis went limp for a second. He was surprised to see Castlebeck closing rapidly on Calitri without even being aware of how near his quarry was. Castlebeck knocked over a pipe with a loud *clang*. Calitri turned, thinking it was Memphis, and fired at the shape he saw. Memphis finally managed to pull himself to the walkway as he heard voices.

"Who are you?" asked Calitri, his gun still trained on Castlebeck.

Castlebeck's heart was pounding after the shot narrowly missed him. He flashed his badge. "Long Beach P.D.! Raymond Calitri, you are under arrest!"

Calitri advanced with his gun held high, pointed right at the detective's head. "You're in the wrong country," he told Castlebeck. "It's England where the coppers don't carry guns."

Castlebeck had to talk fast. "Calitri, you're not stupid. Walk out with me, and you have options. Bail, house arrest, fancy lawyers trying to plea-bargain your ass. But kill a cop, and your life is over."

"You've got that backwards, surely," Calitri said, his voice full of menace. "I kill a cop, and *your* life is over. Not all bad, though. Think of the funeral. It'll be on the telly. Everyone out there, dressed and pressed, guard of honor. Twenty-one–gun salute and the fucking Stars and Stripes draped over your coffin. Doesn't get much better than that. It'll be the greatest day of your life."

Castlebeck's eyes froze on Calitri's hand

around the gun, watching the fingers squeeze, waiting for the noise—

Bang! The gun fired as Memphis threw himself into Calitri from the intersecting walk, causing him to miss and plowing him against the balustrade. The rail and the balusters gave way, and Calitri fell, his face a mask of surprise, shock, and sorrow all the way down, four stories, *slam!* onto a case of mahogany.

Raymond Calitri was sprawled dead on the coffin meant for Kip.

Memphis and Castlebeck stood on the catwalk and stared, first at Calitri and then at each other. Sirens wailed in the distance—Castlebeck's backup was on the way.

"I'll go quietly," Memphis said.

Castlebeck frowned. "Well, well. Here I am—smack-dab in the middle of a moral dilemma, Randall. I've got to look deep into my soul on this one. You've torn the town to shreds with that little chase. And I've been after you as long as I can remember. Yet—I appreciate what brought you here. A brother's love, et cetera. And you just saved my life. . . . And you did get rid of a chicken bone down the throat of our fair city. So what to do?"

They could hear cruisers pulling in, the sirens

winding down. "I can't help you with this one, Detective," Memphis said.

There was a long pause.

"Go," Castlebeck said. "Get outta here, Raines. I'll clean this up."

Memphis hesitated, not sure whether to believe. As with Eleanor, he and Castlebeck had a history.

"You're sure?" Memphis asked.

"Not sure at all. Got a sour stomach," Castlebeck confessed. "But you better get your ass out of here before I change my mind."

Memphis smiled, turned to go, then stopped and looked back at the detective. "There's a container ship at Pier Fourteen. Should sweeten your stomach."

Castlebeck nodded. And Memphis was gone.

15

In the parking lot outside Otto's, Donny Astricky raised the hood of an old Pontiac billowing smoke, revealing the car's recent conversion to a barbecue pit. Donny was armed with a brush and tongs and protected by an apron that read CHAIRMAN OF THE CHARCOAL.

"Pork shoulders are up!" he announced.

Tumbler was first in line with a paper plate. The others followed, and soon they were all feasting at picnic tables. Sway generously helped Toby cut his food before he made too much of a mess.

"Poor Toby," Freb said. "He looks like he's in a lot of pain."

"Pain, my ass," said Mirror Man, watching Sway. "You can cap me next!"

Suddenly the Sphinx cleared his throat, which drew everyone's attention.

"If Toby's unpleasant wounding has, in some way, enlightened the rest of you as to the grim finish below the glossy veneer of criminal life and inspired you to change your ways, then his injury carries with it an inherent nobility and a supreme glory. We should all be so fortunate. You can say, 'Poor Toby.' I say, 'Poor us.' "

Tumbler, Mirror Man, and Donny stared, dumbfounded. Then Mirror Man took off his sunglasses for the first time and said, "Say something else, man!"

But the Sphinx had lapsed back into silence again, devouring a baby-back rib.

A car pulled up, occupied by a couple of detectives from downtown. Memphis walked over to greet them.

"Normally," Castlebeck, the driver, said, "a congregation of car thieves in my district would chap my ass."

"That's not what this is," Memphis said. "This is a celebration of rehabilitation. Otto's offered me and Kip gainful employment." He proudly pointed to a new sign over the shop:

HALLIWELL AND RAINES
AUTO RESTORATION

"I'm glad for you and Kip," Castlebeck said. "Just make sure your other friends don't cause me to regret I looked the other way at the scrapyard."

"I know, I know," Memphis said. "If I even tear the little under-penalty-of-law-this-is-not-to-be-removed tag off a mattress, you'll be all over me."

Sway came up with barbecue for the men in the car.

"Thank you," Castlebeck said. "I gotta tell you, Memphis, while you represented everything I'm against, you did it stylishly."

"A world without style, Detective, is no good for anyone."

"Catch you later," Castlebeck said, pulling away.

Memphis put his arm around Sway and walked back to the barbecue. Kip came up to him with a small box. "Listen, man, I got something for you," he said.

Memphis took the box. "What is it?"

"Open it."

Memphis did, revealing a set of car keys. "Keys are good. What do I do with them?"

Then everyone looked at Otto, standing by a tarp-covered car. "And now, ladies and gentlemen," began Otto, clearly loving the moment, "it gives me great pleasure to present . . ." He nodded to Junie, who helped him pull the tarp off—

Another Eleanor.

"She's in the pupa stage," Otto said. "Still under restoration. Hasn't got the right seats, the right paint yet. Give us a few weeks and she'll burst from her chrysalis as a majestic butterfly."

Memphis gasped.

"Hey, why don't you get in—turn her over?" suggested Atley.

So Memphis got in. Atley shut the door and leaned on it, waiting for Memphis to start her up.

"Look, man," Memphis said quietly, "I know what you did for me. Thanks."

Then he turned the key. The engine hummed to life, and he revved her. She sounded great.

"Of course, I took a little time to work some magic on the engine," Otto said modestly.

Someone turned on the music, and Otto grabbed Junie. As the two of them danced, and the others cheered, Memphis drove the new Eleanor around to Sway.

"You want to go for a ride?"

She came to the door and got in, smiling. "Sure."

And off they went.

As they roared off, Memphis noticed Sway watching the speedometer as he pushed it way past the legal limit. "What do you like best—speeding or having sex?" he asked her. And he grinned, patting the seat next to him.

Sway moved closer. "How about speeding while having sex?"

And before the people in Otto's yard lost sight of Eleanor, she swerved once before straightening out and tearing away.